DIARY OF
A RENTAL CAR

Tales of Travel, Humor, and Life as Told Through the
Perspective of a Rental Car.

Jim McAllister

Edited by Alex Halverson

Cover design by Xee_Designs1

Author photograph by Dennis Quinn

"

"What is the difference between a tank and a rental car? There are some places you will not drive a tank."

- Unknown

Contents

Initial Thoughts

Befo reading this book, you need to take it with a grain of salt. The title alone for this should be a dead giveaway. I will try to explain it as best as I can. Bear with me here. This idea came to me when I was on a road trip with my older brother Rick. See, I have had the fortunate experience of doing a good amount of traveling throughout my life, and a considerable portion of it by car. Traveling is something that I truly enjoy, and I have always loved a good long drive. Just to see the country, add experiences, make new memories, and spend time with people important to me. I have always preferred a road trip over flying. Maybe it is my love of exploring or watching the changing scenery go by; different parts of the country that I have never seen, or places I have been to before and always enjoyed going back to. Stopping at any attraction that should come around. Even as a kid, I loved looking at the mileage signs as a countdown to my destination; always enjoying what was in between. Flying has you stick to a strict schedule, horrible, overpriced food, and few options to make detours if you want to. Sure, that is the way to go for a long distance and limited time. That being said, I love the freedom that a road trip provides.

What had me thinking about this concept was when Rick took me out to Las Vegas for a weekend, to hang out and spend time together. It was during a time in my life that I truly needed it, and he has always kept me grounded. Rick and I have put thousands and thousands of miles on rental cars, and I cannot think of any trip we took that we did not have a good time. There have been so many trips the two of us have taken I honestly do not think I could recall all of them. We do not even need to be on vacation together to have fun. We can have a great time at the grocery store with each other.

On that particular trip home to Phoenix, we started talking about the car we were in. Pointing out the color, comfort, trunk space, daily price, and most importantly, the ability for me to lean the passenger seat back as I was slightly overserved at the bar the night before. Things as you get older become conversations. He took the liberty of renting a car on this run as my truck at the time was old, completely unreliable, averaging about nine miles to the gallon, and leaking fluids like a Soviet submarine. We talk about everything and anything on our road trips. Important things, unimportant things, everything. I also have a general tendency to never shut up and talk all the time; a "chatterbox" is a conservative description. My mom said once I learned to talk, I just kept going with it, never stopping for over forty years since. There is a lot of truth to that statement. I never shut the hell up.

The way back on that trip from Las Vegas, I remember asking Rick something of the sort, "What if this car could tell its story?" Maybe it was the hangover talking as we did just leave Las Vegas. I remember him looking a bit of confused at my question, probably wondering if I had, in fact, continued drinking that morning. He was possibly too hungover to proceed with any follow-up questions and just did not care. Perhaps. I did get one or two more in before our departure that morning? The mystery remains. It was just something I was thinking about as we were headed back home, and I really could not shake the thought. Eventually, I clarified, meaning, what if this car could actually keep an account of its first couple of years? A "diary" if you will.

Rental cars have so many drivers doing so many different things. That is a lot of different experiences outside of just the same person going to the same places every day. A rental car is in new places with new people all the time. What would this car see? Where has this car been? How many memories were created in this car? What will be its story? How would it talk about its journey? Does it develop a personality based on the experiences it will go through? Rick seemed somewhat intrigued. Or at least humored me. Probably the latter. After scouring the internet for a shorter amount of time than I should have, I was able to conclude that I may be the first one to think of this subject. Or at least put enough effort into writing a book about it. Thus, the concept of this book was born.

Full disclosure on something. Embarrassing now, but transparent as I believe the truth is critical. Cards on the table. In my youth, I was a complete and utter bastard to rental cars. You received a relatively new car at your disposal for a minimal amount of money. Failing bringing it back with any visible damage and still running, one essentially had a free pass to abuse the vehicle to their heart's morbid desires. I will neglect to mention any specifics of what I have done in said youth, even though I believe the statute of limitations has run out, but if we have been all wrong about religion and when judgment comes and we are created and judged by the machines and not a higher power, I am completely and absolutely 100% fucked in the afterlife for what I have done. Not likely, but anything is a possibility. I rule nothing out.

Let us just say that "jumping" a vehicle does not have the same outcome as what is portrayed on television. Nowhere remotely close. I still cannot believe I did that. I brought it back and somehow did not get charged extra. I genuinely feel bad for whoever acquired that vehicle down the line.

I am much older now and generally speaking treat rental cars the same as my own vehicles if not better. From my understanding, after the two year or so life cycle, a car starts at a rental company, these vehicles are generally sold off and that will probably be someone's first newer and reliable car. Be good to rental cars, people. Do not be me back then. Maybe that recent college grad, a young family getting started, or someone like me now, that is extremely frugal and always tries to save a few bucks, are the ones buying these vehicles. We should be good to these cars for that alone. Do not wreck it for the next person. If that car somehow had a voice and could spend a couple of hours telling stories of what they had seen, they would curse me to the deepest and most uncomfortable bowels of hell. Like an old man sitting on their porch with a corn cob pipe instilling wisdom upon you. What were the most memorable experiences it had? What would they say? What stood out the most for them? What if the car even developed its own personality based on these experiences?

Maybe this is a story that would have been told.

1.

My Start. Beginning Of Life as A Car.

It finally came. My day was finally here! I became a completed, fully functional car. The final day came, from the beginnings of my frame being molded from raw steel out of Pennsylvania to the precise installation of all my plastic and electronic components. I am rolled off the end of the line at the assembly plant, the last stage. The new car smell we all had at this point. I remember hearing workers talking about this, in the previous phase, where I went through the visual inspection and was rolled off to the final portion of this process before being shipped off and sold.

My tires touched the cement for the first time. Not a speck of break dust on my wheels. The sound of my ignition being started for the first time, my voice to the world that I am complete. Slowly driven to a new area of the assembly plant, not a single noise is out of place. I function flawlessly. All the belts running in perfect harmony with my engine. My transmission shifts as smooth as can be. Every bolt, every screw, tightened perfectly.

I looked up to see the guy I had seen many times before, a face emotionless through his safety glasses half staring at his clipboard and a half looking disapproving look at everything else. I do not mean just cars. I mean everything in life. It was my first experience with someone who did not care about anything this early into my creation; however, it was something I knew of. After a few minutes of him walking around checking the gaps between body panels and reading another inspection report, he gave me the final check on my documents, and I was off. Day one of my life as a fully functional driving vehicle was finally here.

I was ready. Or so I thought.

I was eager to hit the road! Everything was new, everything on me worked, and nothing was worn out. I was brand frigging new, and I could not wait for where I am going! With pristine navy-blue exterior paint, and a tan cloth interior with matching door panels, the most boring-looking four-door mid-size sedan in creation, ready for the adventure of life. Two cup holders in the front, and two on the back, lumbar support in my driver's seat, and cruise control features right on the steering wheel. No rear air conditioner. Fake black leather wrapped around the steering wheel. My odometer was showing 0.5 at this time.

I wondered where was I going, who would share their life with me? I couldn't wait! I really hoped I would go to a good home, maybe bought by someone who was just out of college and secured their first "real" job, and I would be their first new car. I look forward to the picture of them at the dealership, holding up the keys, completely excited at their purchase of me. The memory of the first new car they bought their entire lives, long after my parts rusted. Oh, maybe I would go to a young family and get to take their kids to school in the morning, take the parents to work and in the afternoons drop the kids off and pick them up at football and guitar lessons, get to hear all about their day on the way home and be put in a garage at night in the suburbs. I wanted to be there with them as their lives continued to grow. Wow, I may even be a daily driver for someone famous. Sure, that was reaching, but in life, all things are possible.

While being packed on to a train, my new location and owner were made obvious pretty early. My fate was written as delivery paperwork fixed to the windshield. I was being sent to Phoenix, Arizona. A city I have heard that was so hot in the summer it is a testament to the arrogance of humans in setting up living arrangements that no man, or be it machine, should ever have to exist in. On top of that, I was sold off to a car rental company. That means I would have a new ass in the seat every few days. A slave to somebody new every few days. No real true home to call my own.

I am pissed off!

The train ride was uneventful out west. A few days go by, locked inside a metal tomb with little light coming through or wind. I did not even get to see anything on this trip; I just felt the slight shake of the train on the terrain and the sound of metal wheels on the track. All I really had to look at was the car in front of me for three long days. The exact same car I was. Same color. The same car I have heard people refer to as boring family sedans.

Upon delivery, I was taken to a lifeless parking garage. At the airport, nonetheless. Crammed in with hundreds of other similar vehicles. When not being driven around, this would be where I will call home. Rumors circulate that rental cars were typically met with an undesirable path as people driving them have no long-term investment and typically run them harder. By applying the gas and brake pedal with more force than their own vehicles, and some people even find humor in building up their own lives by destroying a small part of mine. Outstanding. I did not know what to make of this. I was not sure how I am supposed to feel. This was so far outside of what I had hoped for.

So early on in life, I was already learning about disappointment, which I will assume will only gain with time.

It was initially sad, really. Having been dropped off late at night in a dark parking garage, not even placed under the lighting to show off my new paint job. A temporary license plate crookedly affixed to the back window with tape. Nobody to celebrate having me as their own personal vehicle. No smiles at the sight of me from a new owner. No rides to show me off to their friends and family on the brand-new car they bought. No bond to be formed early on. Not even parked at a well-lit car dealership to be sold at, fixed with balloons and some unoriginal slogan placed on my windshield to entice buyers like "Brand New!" or "This could be yours!" No real homecoming for me. Ready to conquer the world without an owner to do so. This was my first real experience out in the world. I was out there alone.

But maybe, I considered, this would not be all that bad, though. I heard stories of rental cars living the dream despite the negatives that go with it. Being taken out on vacations, unforgettable road trips, and epic adventures. Who knows what I might see?

I tried to remain optimistic. I needed to.

As a testimony to my beginning of life, I decided to keep stories of some of the renters who really stood out. This is a very small fraction of people that rented me but ones I really remember well. Maybe they taught me a lesson, made me laugh at how incredibly asinine they were, or some really great adventures I had during this phase of my existence. My diary if you will. These are a few of the ones that really stood out to me.

2.

The Deer Hunter

"Would you like to add insurance to the car?" the rental agent asked the guy as they did the walk-around car inspection before leaving.

"Yeah, I think I am going to need it." He responded with little hesitation. Such a quick response to this question has always had me nervous, because I had already learned that to a renter, insurance was a free pass to essentially do whatever the hell you want to the car and not be charged for it or have your insurance rates go through the roof. No deductible. Blame it on somebody else. The "I have no idea how the entire bumper was ripped off" situation. It is the sum of all my fears to jump at that option so quickly without a conversation about the cost or exact coverage.

He took the clipboard from the rental agent, initials the enormous number of appropriate boxes for the additional charge, and he was off.

This guy was tall, and after leaving the rental lot, he drove pretty quickly. Stepping on the gas at yellow lights, never really making a complete stop at any of the posted stop signs. He spent a ridiculous amount of time looking at directions on his phone of where he was going without looking at the road ahead. He spat tobacco into an empty soda can, every other deposit not completely getting the waste into the can but dripping off his chin where the remnants were wiped from his hand on-to the side of my driver's seat. Beautiful. Just because you agreed to an additional $32 a day for the insurance, it's not a license to prematurely end my usefulness.

After the familiar tones from the most annoying voice on the planet of the electronic GPA lady constantly saying, "Turn right here, turn right here," we finally arrived at our destination on the outskirts of Phoenix. Not quite in the sticks, but well outside of the suburbs. Far east from town.

It was a ranch-style house, with no paved driveway and a sign that said, "I don't dial 911, I dial .357!" attached to the chain link fence with the remnants of a coat hanger. An older house, but a comfortable looking one. A large front patio and a few dead bushes hang from planter boxes by the front door. Honestly, this was the sort of place I liked. Good folks who usually wanted to have a good time. Even if he drove like a complete asshole on the way up there, as I was subjected to.

He pulled up to a few people sitting outside by a small fire in a pit right in the center of the front yard. It looked like it was made from an old washing machine drum. Beside the house was a boat that looked like it had not been out on the water for well over a decade. Getting out, he was greeted by the ten to twelve people there with a lot of hugs, and a cold beer was opened and given to him. No less than eight dogs came running out of the house and one of them walked up to my back right tire, relieving itself with a healthy stream of urine. Lovely.

I waited for someone to get the garden hose out and take care of that situation. Even a quick rinse. Nope. Guess that it's my problem, huh?

They sat around for a few hours, drinking beer, laughing, drinking beer, having something cooking on the BBQ outside that smelt amazing, drinking beer, telling jokes, drinking beer, catching up, and drinking beer. I saw a virtual gold mine of aluminum cans for their recycle value in a plastic bin that was empty only a few mere hours ago. It was quite an impressive feat to consume that amount of alcohol in such a short amount of time. But they were all catching up and having a good time. Being a car and all, I have never experienced being drunk, but it looked like a hell of a good time. I'm glad they were together. I always like seeing people together and enjoying their time. However, it's probably best that I cannot get drunk, being a car and all. That irony was not lost on me. The whole driving thing and all.

After a few hours of them catching up and urinating on every square inch of the trees surrounding the home and two events of me getting a golden shower I was still pretty upset about, they retreat for the evening inside the house with the promise of getting up early for their trip the following day. As much as they were talking, I did not know what the plans were for the next day. Only that they would wake up a few hours before the sun was to come up. I was not much of an early riser, but I was curious to see what the plans for the next day. Maybe build a bathroom inside the house because I didn't recall anyone going inside to use one. Who knows?

The next morning, four hours after the sun rose and well behind the agreed-upon time to meet back up, I saw a pickup truck drive up to the property. The kind of truck you could tell was originally red when it was new thirty years ago, but the decades of getting burned by the Arizona sun turned it to a color more closely resembling the dirt around us. The big old truck that just screams America, with a seven mile-to-the-gallon battle cry. The kind of truck with stories to tell. I wanted to hear those kinds of stories. It would be like listening to an elder on the key to a great life. Even long after this trip, I still wonder what stories that truck could have told me.

I become a bit envious, wishing for a brief period that I had been built as a truck. Go out and do truck things, you know? The guy who rented me comes out the front door; he'd probably only been awake for no more than one or two minutes, eyes puffy and red from the night before holding a cup of coffee. The guy in the truck gets out and gives a huge hug to the guy who rented me. I was unable to make out their relationship completely the night before. I assume, due to the obscene amount of beer they drank and the profanity-laced conversation that took place with it, but I could confirm that they were brothers and grew up in the house we were at together. The guy who rented me had moved for a job, years back and truly missed being at home and missed his brother. They had been planning this trip together for the last few months, saved their money for a long time and were ready to have a quality experience together.

Since their heads were a bit clearer this morning instead of last night, I was able to confirm what the agenda was and what their plans were. They were both drawn for a deer hunt up in northern Arizona.

Great! I figured they would head out and come back after a day or two with a nice harvest of game meat after having a great time together, and they would make great memories together in his brother's truck. Excellent! I would just be here, waiting for the guy who rented me to come back, take him to his return at the airport and that will be that. Yet, I was quick to learn they had other plans. That was to take me up and not the truck.

I drew this conclusion when his brother started to take hunting gear out of his truck and place it in my trunk: a top-shelf .308 bolt-action rifle, backpack, game processing materials, and two coolers filled with ice. The guy who rented me came out of the house, put his bag in my trunk, and both of them gave a hug and a wave to their parents on the front porch, wishing them off for a successful hunt.

While I can assume this is not the first time it has been done, a front-wheel drive four-door sedan is probably not the pick of the litter as the best hunting vehicle. In terms of a hunting trip, I should be the awkward kid who was picked last at a game of flag football in a middle school setting for this task. You do not select the four-foot kid for basketball when you have plenty of six-foot kids to select from. Why would you take me when you have a first-round draft pick literally parked right next to me?

When the drive began, I learned that I was the vehicle for this trip because my gas mileage was better than the old truck. Well, save our natural resources, I guess.

We began the drive up north, only two hours up into the mountains and I must say I am relieved that our only offroad excursion was a well-grated dirt road with very few bumps and clear of all major rocks and any other debris. I was sweating that whole drive because the guy who rented me *did* purchase insurance. We pulled up to a makeshift campsite, nothing professionally built. A small patch of dirt with trees cleared out and a campfire ring built with rocks locally sourced, from the best I can tell, and another area just big enough to pitch a tent. They arrived, got set up, and started to talk about their plans for tomorrow. To get up before the sun rose, scout a nearby field, and with some luck, execute a deer in the morning, and be on their way.

This was when a burgeoning number of questions came to mind. If this hunt was successful, we would fit all the hunting gear, coolers, weapons, and other essentials into me? If this did go to plan the one thing I could not wrap my head around, no matter how it played out, always came back to the same question...

Where the fuck was the deer supposed to go? Seriously. I wondered if they were going to prop it up in the backseat and put a little hat on it so they could use the carpool lane? Strap it to the roof? My owner's manual has a lot of information in it but nothing about transporting a carcass of this size. Or any carcass for that matter. Even if they dump the food from the coolers, I fail to believe that it is mathematically feasible to chop up the corpse and disburse the meat into those receptacles.

I do regress, because as a car, I have few natural enemies. Depending on where I am at, rust is one of them. Other cars or vehicles running into me, that is another big-ticket item. Also, drunk drivers. I hate them. Another one that circled around in the water cooler talk with cars are deer. Those bastards jump out with little to no notice and have enough mass to completely destroy a car when hit at cruising speed. Damn forest rats. Sure, the impact usually kills the deer, but also me, the car. Nobody walks away winning. It is like communism. It looks great on paper, but in the real world everybody loses. One less deer on the planet is one less I have to worry about running into.

I will give these two credit that night. They spent a few hours up after the sun went down, drinking soda and talking about all the good times and things they did together when they were younger. Just reminiscing on old times and how happy they were able to make this trip come to fruition. They talked about hunting trips when they were younger, all the great things their parents did for them, and everything else that had been happening in their lives the last few years during the time they could not see each other. It was great being outside of Phoenix with these two, among the pine trees and nature. There's something so much different here than the city. That cool breeze coming by every few minutes. It just felt like time moves much slower there than anywhere else. Unlike the previous night, they went to bed at a very reasonable hour to get ready for their hunt early the next morning.

Well before sunrise, I heard the sounds of them waking up in the tent. The grunts people make in the first minute of each day. From their tent, I heard more cursing than most people have in this process, but to each their own. Cars do the same thing in different weather and age. They emerged from their tent, while it was still dark outside, and the brother brought a pot up to a small gas stove to start the first pot of coffee for the two of them. The strong aroma of coffee brewing overtook the pine scent around us, and he poured two large sealed cups for himself and the guy who rented me. They quickly packed up their hunting gear, and the brother slung his rifle on his shoulder, bringing his hands up to his mouth to warm them up by blowing on them. And as quick as they packed up without saying much, they were off into the woods.

Not much happened over the next hour or so. I sat there and slowly watched the sun rise from the east. It felt cold enough that if it were to rain, that might turn into snow. The woods started to come alive as a small breeze came through, making the pine needles in the trees dance a little. It had a feeling of calm that was so relaxing. The rising sun was starting to warm the dew that had set out on my hood, roof, and trunk. I could practically hear the warmth of the sun thaw out what had frozen overnight. It was quiet. It was peaceful. I liked it. I especially liked having a new experience to add to my short life thus far.

The sun had just fully risen giving birth to a new day. As much as a car like me should not be that far out into the woods, for a brief period of time, I was glad I was there to see it. I got out of my comfort zone as a city car, and became a country car. As I sat there basking in the rising sun enjoying the cool mountain air, it was quickly disrupted by the loud crack of that .308 rifle in the distance. Probably three-hundred to four-hundred yards from me. Only to be followed up by the sounds of excitement from the guy who rented me and his brother. With what I can assume were the celebrations and high-fives and a multitude of congratulations for the kill, it brought me back to the same question I had earlier. Where in the hell is the deer going to go on the way back?

Twenty or thirty minutes later, the two of them emerge into my view walking up a bit of a hill. A deer was being dragged from a tarp by the two of them back to the campsite. Its lifeless body made me question my own mortality as, at some point, I would resemble this animal when I am brought to my final resting place. What I have heard is called a "junk yard." Where people would come from all over and molest my remains and harvest any usable parts to prolong their own vehicles for a brief period of time longer. That whole thought always creeped me out.

They spent the next two hours or so processing the deer and organizing all the parts of this animal into what was usable and what was not. Like skilled surgeons, these two had me impressed with this process. Communicating without complete sentences, they seemed to know what each other needed help with. Clearly, it was not their first rodeo. I also learned what the two coolers full of ice were for. The usable meat. Excellent. Earlier in this trip, I was concerned about the animal riding "shotgun" somewhere inside me. I was going to take back everything I said about these two on their respect for me. Like a game of serial killer Tetris, they were able to fit all the usable meat into the two coolers. Bravo. I was almost 100% proud of these two until they came to the last decision on what to do with "the head."

I learned that the brother wanted to mount "the head" of this animal in his living room. Sure, I get it. As cars, we have hood ornaments. Nowhere near the same, but I get it. Status symbol. After carefully processing the meat and placing it into the coolers and into the backseats, they stood there, lording over the head of this animal, doing their best to devise a plan. I learned that they had an appointment with a taxidermist, which I was able to devise on my own is an individual that will take an animal that was once alive, now dead, and make the dead animal look like it busted through a wall and is looking around like cover art to an alternative band photo shoot. Yet, they had to figure out what to do with the head before arriving at said taxidermist. The coolers were already too full; even if they threw out the meat, this head was way too big to fit in one. Once I started liking these two and giving them credit, they made a decision that had me throwing out my impression of them and go back, due to improper plan management about the head of this deceased animal.

After a quick measurement, they decided to put the coolers in the back seat and the head in my trunk. OK. In theory this plan would have worked except an overlooked factor is that even when dead, an animal that had its head cut off will still continue to bleed. Not much, not much at all, but enough to cause a problem. Watching them attempt to put the head in a garbage bag to contain the blood loss was met with failure after failure. Six failures to be exact. I also learned if you are going to contain a head inside of a garbage bag, do not buy them from the dollar store. Six bags in the box, six attempts, six failures. The "F" word was used by the two well over six times in this process. The weight of this severed head far exceeded the tinsel strength of the bags. I guess you can't get anything for a dollar anymore. Just spend the extra money. Buy quality garbage bags. Certain things you just should not cheap out on.

After twenty minutes of this shit show, they get an idea to line my trunk with the bags, all six of them, failing to remember they are ripped. They said that should at least be "All right." I would tip my hat to them if I could. They lined the trunk as best as they could, but all liquids take the path of least resistance. Once the head was set inside, I instantly felt blood drain out through every hole in the garbage bags. It leaked into the carpet inside my trunk. Dripping into the spare tire compartment. Come on guys, there is no way this can ever be properly cleaned out later. Then I really saw it, oh God, the deer head, the eyes are open, its fucking eyes were open! It was frigging looking at me! The tongue is partially hanging out.

The drive back was the same as the guy who rented me had done the entire time, heavy on the gas, heavy on the brakes, and taking turns pretty quick. I was not sure if he knew that these motions had the head banging and rolling around in different positions all over my trunk It caused more blood to run out with each motion. I could even hear the blood and other fluids sloshing around in my spare tire compartment, mixing up into the smoothie from hell. Why were the eyes still open on this thing? Couldn't they have taped spare change over them or something?

After two hours of that nightmare drive back, we finally arrived back at the ranch house. They unloaded everything from inside the car first, getting to my trunk last. Might as well just let it all completely drain out in my trunk, right? The entire family bears witness to the kill as my trunk opens up. I figured they would have been quick to take the head out. Nope. Five of them, just stared right at it, commenting on it. Talking about what to name it. After a few minutes, they finally removed the head and carried it somewhere inside the house. Where it went, I have no idea and I still do not care. The vision of that body-less head with eyes wide open and the tongue sticking out will continue to haunt me forever.

I saw the man, who I learned previously was the "Dad" of the two, start to peel back the garbage bags and saw the poor job they did working as a liner. "Look at this, boys. Blood drained all over the trunk of this thing. Y'all to clean that out. Shit. They gonna charge you."

The guy who rented me and the brother went to the side of the house and retrieved a garden hose. Great, I thought, you can bring that out to hose blood out of my trunk but not when the dogs are constantly pissing all over me. In a terrible display at any sort of real effort to clean my trunk properly, they just stood next to it, spraying water inside with enough force to make it splash out of the back. I figured they thought if they kept diluting it enough like that, eventually, it would just be water coming out only. There was a small drain inside my trunk, and I was glad they found it, even if it was obviously not designed for this situation. They also put a few of the little pine tree air fresheners under the spare tire compartment, I assumed was their logic they that if there was any blood leftover, it would be a few days before it would start to stink the entire vehicle up and become the next person's problem. They looked at their clean-up and both deem it to be "good enough" and went about their business

3.

The Three Horrible Renters

I knew these three were going to be trouble when I saw them walking up to me. They all looked about the same age, in their early twenties. One was wearing a soccer jersey from a defunct team, knock-off tennis shoes, and constant use of the word "bro." The second guy, probably one hundred pounds soaking wet, six whiskers I speculate he was attempting to pass off as a beard, and he wore a beanie in almost 100-degree weather. Our third contestant was wearing a pink golf shirt, collar all the way up, and sporting a mullet. He probably thought the mullet was funny. It's not. I had dubbed them "Soccer Jersey", "Beanie", and "Mullet".

I could hear them walking up from the other side of the building before I was able to see them. Please, please, please, keep walking, I hoped desperately. Do not be for me. Then my lights flashed, and my doors unlocked from the remote key. Yup, this festival of jackassery was all mine.

They pile in like children, Soccer Jersey in my driver's seat, Beanie in my passenger seat, and Mullet in the back. Mullet instantly began to kick Soccer Jersey in front of him, giggling like he was the first person to think of this idea. One most kids tire of at age six. The grime from the parking garage he stepped in had already rubbed off on the back of my seat. Beanie stared to yank on the sun-visor in what I could only think was a bid to bend it or break it off. We were not even out of the parking lot at that point.

"Hey, be cool until we are out of sight, just be cool." Soccer Jersey said to the other two. I knew then they were going to do something bad to me. Not only did I have a feeling, but as soon as those car doors were shut, they gave high fives to each other and said they could not wait to completely fuck this car up. Me.

I suddenly and clearly understood why they always kill off the college-age kids in horror movies.

They pull out to the exit of the parking garage normally. Soccer Jersey handed their paperwork to the gate agent; he looked it over and checked the identification of the driver. If only I could speak and say something to him. These guys are going to beat the hell out of me. Why couldn't my battery die now, a flat tire, check engine light, something to have them get a different car? The gate attendant nodded and wished them well. To my disappointment, which would soon be horror, they drove off. Once the window was up, Beanie started to giggle like a school girl again.

Not even one mile away, just out of sight from the building, Soccer Jersey yelled out, "Hold on, assholes!" and stomped on my gas pedal.

The RPM's rev reached the redline, gear after gear, and they holler out with enjoyment. It was not like I was designed to be the fastest car on the road. This clearly was not going to be an easy three days. Just as they got up to speed on this empty road, Soccer Jersey stomped on the brake pedal as hard as he could. My tires screeched, and smoke rolled off them, just to get close to stopping, then slammed on the gas pedal again, repeating this process for the better part of five minutes. The three never stopped laughing at this. Gas, brake, gas, brake, and these jerks could not seem to get enough of it. This was not doing any favors to my brakes.

They head out on the highway, and in between the hysterical laughter and words which I cannot fully translate, I learned that we were going to a college football game the following day, but that evening we were going to a party near the University. Boy, I couldn't wait. Even a car can be sarcastic, which I will continue to learn well.

They were driving around aimlessly. Clearly, none of these three dinks knew how to use a map because they were just guessing at a location to go to in a city they had never been to, constantly slamming on the gas pedal; or where Beanie randomly pulled up my emergency brake at highway speeds. Laughing every time it locked up the back wheels, every time it took more and more rubber off my tires. Alien abductions were said to make thousands of people disappear every year. I would ask fate why they did not select these three, but I assumed the aliens would want nothing to do with them either.

The next hour was pure torture. All they would say is things like, "Hey, dude, no visible damage!" while kicking the door panels, the dashboard, and seats. Mullet, in the back seat, kept elbowing the arm rest in between the two seats, causing a small dent in the material.

Beanie opened my glove compartment, took out the owner's manual, and spat the most ungodly ball of phlegm inside the glove compartment. He opened up the manual to the middle and promptly started ripping pages of it out, throwing them out the window. Not that he was looking, but they were the important ones, fuse diagrams, fuel information, and the like. About half of the manual was spread out on the interstate. I had not even mentioned the littering aspect of this. As if that was not bad enough, he took out a marker and started to write on the other pages left in the manual. Penis drawings, a lot of them. I mean a lot. This guy seemed obsessed with male genitalia. Other than a few occasional curse words written on other various pages, he seemed content and placed the manual back in the glove compartment, right on top of the still-warm ball of phlegm he had deposited there recently. The only thing that hurt more than that was listening to them talk.

When these prodigies finally figured out they were in the wrong part of town, they did not seem to care. They took another hour to beat the living hell out of me some more, somehow without tiring themselves out at all, either. Soccer Jersey finally realized they were defeated and pulled up directions on his phone. Could have solved that by paying extra for the navigation unit offered, but I am sure they would have tried to break that piece of equipment, so maybe it was best it was not purchased as an add-on.

When stopped at a parking lot to get the right directions, Mullet giggled, rolled the window down, and threw the floor mats from the backseats out of the car. Why?

Soccer Jersey, Beanie, and Mullet spent the last 30 minutes of the drive before arriving talking about how they were going to get so drunk and score with so many ladies. I bet one of those is true and it will be the option that has nothing to do with the ladies.

Through some of the worst driving I had seen, we finally arrived at their party destination just before sundown. And by party, it was a house just outside of the University. Techno music was playing, idiots all around dancing with glowsticks, an unkept yard, and every few seconds, the childish "Yeahhhhh!" was thrown out while someone took a shot of alcohol. Milk crates used as seating and furniture.

Beer kegs covered the yard, and red plastic cups were thrown about everywhere. There was not even a garbage can in sight. One guy by the garage was wearing a woman's sundress. Why? All three of my passengers exited me; Mullet slammed my door so hard getting out that the inside door panel is now loose. I was depreciating faster than the parent's investments of college tuition for these three. Upon their arrival, I learned that the owner of this home hosting the "event" is a high school friend of Soccer Jersey. He greeted Soccer Jersey while wearing a toga. They embraced in a hug that resembled bears fighting over the last scrap of a salmon carcass in the woods near a stream. They said the word "bro" about twenty-five times. I decided to call the friend "Toga". Important to note that, instantly, I was also not a fan of Toga.

It would be amazing if I could filter out the memories of the next few hours, the same way my fuel filter can prevent toxins entering me, but I was not drinking to the excess of beer everybody there was. Nope, I was going to be the only one not blacking out that night. Soccer Jersey kept asking where all the "ladies" were at, and even opened up his wallet to show Toga some condoms he had brought. Peeking at the dates, I saw they had expired a year before. Soccer Jersey and Toga leaned up against me, oblivious to the fact that they were constantly moving and scratching up the paint. Lying to each other about the accomplishments they had made over the last two years. The only real distraction was made by Beanie, who vomited on what would be a lawn if Toga had bothered to maintain his property. Looked like he found his limit for the night.

I figured with the amount of beer they drank, there would be a walk to their motel or even a rideshare. Taxi maybe? Foolish of me to think even one person at this deal would have bothered to stay sober to drive everyone else to where they needed to go. No, about as much though was put into that as how everybody dressed. Which was none. Half-assed.

Soccer Jersey hopped in and slammed on the gas while in park, making a race car noise trying to impress one of the four women that actually bothered to be seen at this soiree. He was looking over at them, smiling. Dude, even I, a four-door sedan, knew they were not impressed. Mullet climbed into my passenger seat with his sunglasses on at 2 in the morning. Beanie was doing his best to compose himself with the vomit fest he had after drinking too much, and barely hobbled into me, scratching his metal studded belt all over the paint while doing so. As assumed, the women were not impressed.

I dreamed up a scenario that the only reason these ladies were here was they were casing the joint to rob it. Or harvest someone's organs, only for them to wake up in what I would guarantee is a tub that has not been cleaned in ages. A note next to them saying, "Sorry about the kidneys, Bro." While lying in a pool of ice after a harvest of their organs. Just waiting for everybody to pass out for their opportunity to do either activity. I hope they do.

Soccer Jersey and Mullet were making small talk in the front while Beanie passed out in my backseat in no less than thirty seconds. Snoring and with every huge breath the few whiskers from his chin, vomit was still glistening on them, dance a little from his exhaling. They talked about how that evening was just the "warm up", and tomorrow would be their night. They were saving it up for then. Yeah, sure. Put all your eggs in one basket, fellas.

I was happy to say that the only smart thing they did was instantly pull out a map to guide them to their motel instead of aimlessly driving around. They were only a couple of miles away, and if we make it there, they were sure to pass out. I would like to say we made it without incident. I would like to say there would be no more damage done to me. I would like to say that would be the end of the childish behavior from these three. There is a lot that I would have liked differently about today. Other than a crash where people or myself are injured, the second worst thing to happen did.

"PUKE!" I heard Beanie yell from the back seat. Slamming his fist into the headliner, putting a crease in that material. When the hell did he wake up, this guy was sleeping like a heavyweight knocked him out. His lightning-fast departure from his slumber and yelling startled Soccer Jersey and Mullet.

"You going to puke?" Soccer Jersey said. I say said because he really did not ask if he was going to puke, in a nonpartisan manner, only related the same word back to him.

Nothing else was said. Apparently, none needed to be. Beanie began to projectile vomit at an alarming rate. Had it not been me getting thrown up in, I probably would have been rather impressed how such a small person can hold, and then dispose of so much liquid. It got everywhere; all over the seats, himself, his shoes, my back window, my door panels, my floor, and even my roof liner. The smell was horrendous. Chunks of half-digested food were in the mix. I suppose I took a small bit of satisfaction as the spray did make its way on to Soccer Jersey.

Hurriedly, Soccer Jersey pulled me off into the nearest gas station at the end of the block. Soccer Jersey and Mullet got out as fast as they could, leaving Beanie behind in the backseat to wallow in his own filth.

Eventually Beanie got out, swearing, and told the other two, "I don't feel so good." No shit? Because what you did constitutes normal behavior? I did not exactly feel all that fantastic right then, either. Knowing this is a situation they need to address, I saw the best coordination of a plan they could bring forth.

Mullet talked to the gas station attendant, and gave him a few bucks. He came out a moment later and hooked up a garden hose they could use. He hooked it up to a water spigot on the side of the gas station. They spent the next few minutes spraying out the vomit as best as they could and wiped other areas out with crumpled up newspaper. They drove to the vacuum area on the other side of the parking lot and did their best to suck up as much water as possible. They were not exactly treating this biohazard with the attention it deserved; at least they were not waiting until tomorrow to figure it out. Not that I forgive any of these actions in any way. The late summer temperature in Phoenix would definitely cook this matter to the point where I would rather be euthanized in one of the car crushers I have heard about. With that, they retreated down the street, where we pulled into undoubtedly the most economical motel lodging available.

Thank God they slept in all morning. In the early afternoon, I saw mullet, now sporting a teal golf shirt with the collar up, drop about twenty dollars into the vending machine outside into energy drinks and junk food. God, this guy sucked. He gave a little too enthusiastic "Sup, Bro?" to another customer sitting outside their room who gave no acknowledgment back; instead, he stared him down like Mullet owed him money. I found humor in that. A couple hours later, the three of them headed out of the room and jumped into me.

"This car still smells like puke," Beanie said. Ya think? "Mullet came up with a brilliant plan to purchase cleaning material that puts a temporary solution to the odor. Not exactly cleaning the vomit, but something to absorb that putrid stench. Enough to be able to turn me in and not get charged anything extra.

From their conversation, I learned we were already heading out to the game, where Toga had a place to tailgate beforehand.

The three went through a Mexican food restaurant on the way over, selecting the least ideal options to eat while in a moving vehicle. The burrito Mullet had was constantly dripped some sort of grease out of the bottom. Instead of putting some napkins under it or finding any sort of adult solution, he moved his leg to the side to let it drop out on to the floor, laughing with his friends at his solution. Since he was in the back seat on this drive, it probably would not have been such a bad thing if my floor mats were not thrown out into a fucking random parking lot the day before. While driving, Soccer Jersey constantly wiped sour cream off onto the side of my seat, even though there were about five hundred napkins in the bag. Beanie was the only one that is actually using the foil wrap to collect the food and grease droppings but fuck him anyway.

The four of them spent about an hour in the parking lot. They parked next to Toga's car and, spent time in the same conversation they had the previous night. Nothing really made complete sense. They drank cheap cans of beer out of brown paper bags while clearly violating the no alcohol allowed signs placed in abundance. Never a better sight to see than them walking off together to go to the game. More than likely to annoy other sports fans around them.

Being newer in my stage as a rental car, in their absence, I pondered how often things like this would happen. How bad can people treat a machine like me and get enjoyment out of it? There was wishful thinking that they would be arrested for something and would leave me to be taken back to the rental car lot with a tow truck. I had a feeling that my luck would not be that great.

It was nice having that time with them gone. Watching other people go into the game with what appeared to be nothing more than having a good time was reassuring. It was a nice break away from these guys.

At the end of the game, the unwelcome sight of the four of them brought a gag reflex I was unaware I was able to possess. They had obviously found a way to obtain more alcohol because these guys all returned as drunk as they had been the night before. Toga tried for a few minutes to convince them to go back to his place for the "after party" as he unzipped his pants and begins to relieve himself on my front right tire. Soccer Jersey joined him on the back right tire, while listening to Toga repeatedly tell him that tonight, he promised there would be many more ladies at the party.

Not to be overdone, Mullet decided to pop the hood my hood and open up the cap to the window washer fluid. He then emptied his bladder inside the best as he could, largely urinating all over my motor and other components under the hood while aiming for the window washing fluid reservoir. Laughing like this is the greatest thing and all else that has been done to me fails in comparison. Mullet walked to my trunk, bending the radio antenna slightly, and spat inside on my backseat.

Beanie just stood there watching like the weak individual I was learning he was. At least his friends, as undesirable as they are, can hold their booze. Not a care in the world for other people walking by and not a law enforcement representative in sight for a proper arrest at indecent exposure. Mind you, there was a portable bathroom not even fifty feet away from us. I gave up a while ago trying to understand these guys.

Soccer Jersey, Muller, and Beanie turn down Toga as they have a very early flight the next morning. Thank God. Despite pleas from Toga, this was one of the better decisions made by my original trio even with the promise of what Toga referred to as a "virtual swimming pool of horny ladies." After what I saw during their bathroom break on me, any ladies that would have made company with these guys would have slapped an "out of order" sticker on their reproductive organs. The only thing smaller than what they displayed was my amount of respect for them. I was not being nice about that, but I also really did not care.

It was a surprising sight to see the three of them exit their motel room the next morning slightly before six. They looked like they were hurting, and I can only hope the oppressive heat and hangovers they were experiencing were worse than they looked. They were wearing the same clothes they had on the day before, so I assumed they slept as long as they possibly could. From our arrival the night before, I calculated they were able to get maybe five hours of sleep at best. Good.

The three of them were mostly silent on the drive back to the airport. A very welcome departing gift for me. The silence that came from these three was more refreshing than a new set of tires would be. They also seemed to be too tired to engage in any final screw-you damage they could do to me. Not that it mattered much, or I forgave them for that, but the last day of just a normal drive back was what I needed.

After dropping me off, they made a quick exit from the rental car lot after handing the key to an attendant. Doing a quick inventory of myself, I recount the damage these three inflicted on me. It was a long list.

The rental car attendant moved me by the automatic car wash station, got in, looked around for a few seconds and said, "What in the hell? I mean…" He stopped, sniffed a bit, and realized something was not right. "This car smells like shit. What the, what the hell?"

I found out they did get charged for stains on the back seat. While I took a bit of satisfaction in knowing they were charged and wish that the extent of the full damages they did to me would have been discovered. Yeah, there were things missed. I still would have rather had no dealings with them.

The juice was not worth the squeeze.

4.

The Honeymooners

This one started out with what I thought would be uneventful. Son of a bitch was I wrong.

This guy showed up by himself, and I was in the same area I usually sit at in the airport rental car lot. Just waiting for the next renter. One thing that stood out about this guy as he was coming up was that he had no bags with him. Even most guys by themselves usually had a backpack, or failing that, a grocery sack with a few pairs of underwear, a couple of t-shirts, maybe a change of pants, a box of condoms that most people who rent me in their mid-twenties usually go unused, and God willing at least a toothbrush. Nope. Not this guy. He jumped in after locating the parking spot, but a little happier than most people.

Guy drove me to the checkout lane and showed his driver's license. I saw he is a local. A suburb outside of the city, and from what I have heard, offers a pretty decent tax break for homeowners. Whatever the hell a tax break means.

As we left the airport, he drove right back to his house. As he was getting close, I could see him cracking a nice, genuine smile about a quarter mile away from where I saw his home address on the driver's license. Yes, I read over people's shoulders. Cars can be a creeper too. As he pulled up to his house, I saw a real pretty lady, standing outside the house. She immediately jumped up and started waving as soon she saw him pulling up closer to the house. Inside the car, he started waving back with the same enthusiasm, just delighted to be pulling up to see her. I wondered what the hell are these two were so excited about. Then it started to make sense when we arrived.

I saw a car in their driveway, a red sports car, and the windows had that writing on it that said, "Just Married!" and streamers, cans, and all sorts of other crap that I assumed their friends tied to the back of the car to draw attention to their situation. Holy. Shit. I was going on their honeymoon!

He pulled me up to the sidewalk, and she ran over to him faster than he could open the door. He was barely even able to put me in park; she gives him a huge hug and an even bigger kiss on the lips.

He smiled back and said, "Hey, the car is good to go, full tank of gas. You ready to hit the road?"

With tons of energy, she smiled at him and said, "I brought the bags downstairs and am ready to go!"

They were so giddy it was almost annoying. Still, they seemed to be having such a great time it was reassuring that people, by nature, just loved being around each other. Most people do. I was good with this, much better than an average traveler that curses for no reason. I have found it preferable to be around more positive people. Happier people also have a tendency not to beat the shit out of me either, which is what I genuinely favor.

The two of them scrambled for their bags as fast as possible; I could tell they were ready to leave quickly to get this trip started. Maybe for the trip or all the honeymoon intercourse that comes with it. Who knows?

I saw a dog in their doorway staring at them, even putting it's paw up at the screen door. Both loaded the bags as quickly as they can and hurry back to the security gate, opening it up to let that animal out. The two of them, still smiling, let this dog run out of their front door and roll around on the grass in the front yard; the dog was smiling as much as I saw the two of them, just happy to be around its family. I could tell this was not some sort of purebred registered dog.

I heard the lady, who at this time I deemed as "Wife", smile down at him, lovingly grab his face and said to him, "You are a good boy. We picked you out of all the other dogs!" The dog smiled right back at her.

The guy, who I call "Husband", knelt down, stared rubbing his ears, and gave him a huge kiss on the top of the head, and said, "Mom and dad are going on a little vacation, but you are in good hands, buddy. Be good. You are a good dog. We have someone watching you when we are gone. Be good." Then he walked the dog back into the house.

I wished this couple would have just bought me outright from the frigging dealership; they were so cool. Kinda cute, too with such positive energy. It was more refreshing than a new coat of wax on my paint. I would have loved to see them live their everyday lives, with me taking them to work, the grocery store, and any other errands they needed to do. Even bringing that dog out on an adventure, shedding and drooling all over my seats. Just watch them live their lives happily together. At least I would get to be with them during this short chapter.

The two of them got into the car, husband in my driver's seat, wife in my passenger seat. Before starting the ignition, he looked over at her and she looked back. They both smiled, the same way they did when he was pulling up. They both leaned over and kissed each other.

His wife said to him, "That was an incredible wedding, but I am so glad that it is over. Now we start our trip!"

The husband lifted his head up, gave a huge sigh of relief, and said, "Yes, great time, but so glad it's done. Honeymoon!"

They both started these screams of laughter, bunched their fists up in balls of excitement and fired up my ignition. Like little kids. This is great, I would get to see the start of their lives as a married couple! Then, it got better. The wife had their itinerary opened and on their seat. I saw where we were going.

Mission Beach, California!

I have always wanted to see the beach and not a picture in a magazine that people leave in me or a cell phone picture of it. No, I actually always wanted to go to the beach, especially in southern California. All those songs written about the place. I do realize that saltwater is basically cancer to me, the small parts of me that are actually metal, but I did not care. I wanted to feel the ocean breeze on me, spread my front doors open, and start to live this west coast dream. Sure, I am a rental car. Do not care. These people were cool, and I wanted to experience the same joy they do. I want to see the waves from the ocean. I wanted to hear what the ocean sounds like.

What was great about this was when they drove off, the wife held out her left hand, and the husband smiled back and put his right hand in hers.

It was a six-hour drive to Mission Beach, and all I heard them talking about were all the memories they had of their lives when they first met up and all the time before they got married. They laughed at some of the dates they had. They talked about all the friends and family that were at their wedding. All the planning that went into that ceremony and how fast the night went by. How they would look for cheap things to do in their neighborhood, not really caring what it was, just happy that they were together. They laughed at a date they went on where the movie was so bad they walked out of it in the middle. I heard them talk about their very first date at a chain Mexican food restaurant, and all of them were great, except the one in their neighborhood.

I heard them talk about that first date, how he drove her there in his beat-up old pick-up truck, and how they spent three hours in the parking lot, well after the restaurant closed and the lights were turned off, just talking and laughing. Getting to know each other more and not wanting that night to end. Just really enjoying being together. It was on that date in the parking lot together that they both knew they wanted to spend the rest of their lives together. They laughed so hard talking about it that I swore it shook my suspension, possibly eliminating two miles per gallon. It was worth it. They were genuinely happy. It was great hearing them talk about the last few years of their lives together and how much fun they have had with their lives so far. I love happy people.

Then, we hit our destination, Mission Beach. I must say, this place was absolutely stunning! They had a place right next to the beach. I was parked fifteen yards from the sand! I could smell the saltwater I longed for. I looked over and saw hundreds of people enjoying themselves. Families with young children making sandcastles, older couples holding hands walking along the waves rolling up on their feet. I could see two brothers, probably in their late thirties, outside together, talking about their cousins wedding the following day and how proud of her they were.

Just people living and enjoying what the day had to offer at the beach.

The husband and wife got their bags out of my trunk and started to head to their hotel. It was a little later in the day. No more than ten yards from me, both of them turned around, and I kid you not, said, "Thank you, car, for getting us here. We will see you tomorrow!" Then they laughed, waved at me, arms around each other, saying how silly they felt talking to a car. They looked at each other the same they did in front of their house and kissed each other. Well, thank you, my husband and wife, my new friends. I was glad we all got here safe. It felt nice to be included.

Morning came and they were up early with the sun. They were dressed much more casually, sporting shorts and t-shirts; they were ready for the adventure of the day. I did not think they had anything mapped out in particular. All the things they had were essentially pamphlets and information on "What To Do!" in the general area. They climbed inside me, and I heard them say their plan was to drive up the coast and see as much as they could. Then do what they wanted to do when they got there, stop if something looked fun and interesting. They planned on sticking to the Pacific Coast Highway as much as possible headed north. Highway 101. They kept the windows down, took in that sea air. Blasting music they were vaguely familiar with in their attempts to sing along with it. They challenged each other to who knew more lyrics than the other. Their first stop brought them to La Jolla, the first place to get breakfast. One of the typical places you would see near the water with an uncreative restaurant name like "Beaches" where they could fill up.

The day had them constantly driving, stopping every twenty or thirty minutes at a scenic overlook of the ocean, where they could get out, take some pictures and enjoy the area. On these stops, they would take short hikes and explore local stores. Every shop they stopped in was another trinket or memento purchased from this journey. Both of them talked about where they thought it would look best in their house or which would be the best gifts for their family and friends. At every stop, I saw the wad of what I assumed was wedding gift cash deplete at a rapid rate. They were having a blast, and it

27

showed. Smiles never faded from their faces.

That was how it was the whole trip up the coast.

Even though they had been at it for most of the day, we finally made it to Oceanside as the sun was getting ready to set. I could tell they were starting to get tired from the day and they talked about finding a nice place to have dinner. They scanned the side of the road, looking for somewhere special to eat together. While all the food they had throughout the day was the quick and easy variety to be able to spend more time exploring, they wanted dinner to be different. Never specifying, they just wanted something special and it showed. Not romantic, just special. Something special to them. Something they will remember on the first full day of this honeymoon. The same as the place they went to on their first date.

Eventually, a small venue appeared in the distance, with a few open parking spaces out in front, right along the water. It had a better view than they place they were staying at in Mission Beach, I give it that. It looked pretty run down, not the best lighting either. But I would say it had a charm to it. I can see why they picked that place. Nothing else like it. It was the kind of place that probably had more repairs needed than the establishment would care to mention, done with hope and duct tape, but I would venture it had some of the best food for miles around. Or at least the best view. I knew they would remember it for a long time to come.

A few minutes later, I saw them seated out on the patio overlooking the ocean the last few minutes of the sun was barely visible over the horizon. It was at that point in the day, right before the sun was no longer visible itself, only the surrounding light as it disappeared. All the tables on the patio had a small candle in the center, and Christmas lights were strung up for additional illumination at a time when Christmas was nowhere on the horizon of upcoming holidays. But that view. That view was amazing. A few boats off in the distance and the sounds of light waves crashing on the beach. There was nobody else out on the patio, only the two of them. Yeah, that was the place. One they will always remember. I watched them there together as the sun dropped all the way over the horizon of the ocean, bringing on the evening.

For the next two days, I stayed put. It was what I had heard them refer to as "Beach Days." The same ritual took place. I would see them leave their room and head out to the ocean, a bag filled with towels, sunscreen, water, snacks, and whatever else they needed. We did not have to explore every day. It was their honeymoon. Who would not want to spend time there at the beach, anyhow? The weather was fantastic, and when I paid attention to them, they were still having a great time together. The beach was packed with other people doing the same thing. Usually, after the day on the water, they would walk around to local places for dinner, coming back after a few hours, still holding hands, still laughing. Always smiling.

We went out halfway through their week to San Diego for a full day. A short drive south of where we were staying at. We ended up at an abundantly crowed town with an unreasonably large number of God-awful terrible drivers. The husband did an exceptional job navigating through this sea of chaos with what looked like little effort. A professional at dodging the inconsideration of others. This day, they saw quite a bit, a lot of local attractions and a lot of shopping. They explored another town they had never been to. Ate local food. All of that. Instead of spending a lot of time in one place, they seemed to have the "Do as much as we can today" approach going to as many places as they could fit in. I was good with that. It allowed me to do the same thing and see the two of them continue to have a great time. Collecting brochures from the places they were discovering to look through for years to come. Exploring as much as they could that day. The next few days it was back to beach days for them. It was still nice. I had a few more days to overlook the ocean with that great view and take a load off. A few more "days off" for me.

It came to the last full day. The day before the inevitable, where they would begin the drive back home the following day. The last full day to do whatever they wanted and not have to look at a clock. The last day to celebrate this honeymoon. About an hour after the sun rose, I saw them emerge from their room, talking about the day and what they wanted to do with it. Both of them scanned down the walkway adjacent to the beach.

The wife said to the husband, "You know, even though we've made short walks from here for food and drinks, we never really walked around here much. I mean… long distances, really exploring this area and what is down the path next to the beach more than a few blocks. I mean, there are tons of bars and restaurants, right? We can get some drinks, get some dinner, and just take our time walking up and coming back together. What do you think?"

The husband took only a few seconds to think about it and said "I'm on board, let's do it! All day! Walk as far as we want, eat and drink when we want. But let's stay right on the water as much as we can."

A mutual agreement was made as quick as the suggestion came up. They went back into the room to gather a couple of things, and that was it. They were on their way. I would be honest if I said I wish we would have driven somewhere. Maybe another trip up the coast next to the ocean as much as we could. Maybe explore some other places, but this was not my trip. A full day of taking their time walking up the beach, gorging on as much food as possible, and washing it down with overpriced cocktails was not the worst idea they could have.

As chatty as these two are, I knew I would probably hear about the days adventure on the way home the following day anyway. With that, they were off, looking as they headed north up the path. I was not going with them, but I knew they would have a great time, and I took some enjoyment in watching them walk away, hand in hand together, to have another great day.

A while later, I could hear them walking back from an evening out. Still laughing, and even though it had only been a week, I thought that maybe these two were more in love than they were at the start of this journey. I was sure of it. I could tell this by the way they were looking at each other and not the alcohol consumed. I have always been able to tell the difference between people in love and people who were just flat-out drunk. It may have only been a week, but the memories they created together during this time will carry them through a lifetime. Thinking about fifty years from now, when they are so old, they cannot do much more than just be together and look back at all the pictures they took on this trip.

They came back, looking tired from the day and holding hands. The wife stopped her husband and said, "This is our last night here. Let's stay and watch the beach for a little while."

He smiled back and walked her over to the bench close to me, the one with the perfect spot to look over the beach. Right on the sand. It was the same place where I had seen a seagull for the first time just days before. Both kicked their shoes off to put their feet in the sand. They sat down, and she laid her head on his shoulder, their arms wrapped around each other. They just sat there, not saying anything for a while. It had already been dark for a while and the beach was pretty much deserted. Very few other people were out that night.

In that moment, I could really feel how great of a week it had been for them; the energy just projected out from this couple who were just sitting there, listening to the waves crash and watching as the water continued to protrude on the beach, only to sweep back out. That lasted for probably thirty minutes until the husband leaned a little closer to hear ear and said, "You know, I'm going to remember this week forever. I know life will get tough from time to time, but as long as we remember this love, we will weather everything. I cannot wait to grow old with you."

She looked up at him, smiled again, dug her head into his shoulder a little bit more, gave a relaxing sigh, and said back to him. "This is the start of our husband and wife chapter."

Without question, I believe those two would have preferred to spend the entire night out there watching the ocean, but tomorrow was it. I needed to be turned back in, and I assumed those two were going back to work, mowing their grass, paying bills, doing laundry, whatever it was people did inside their houses. All journeys like this eventually come to an end. But I knew this trip was exactly what they said it would be, the start of their husband and wife story. All the pictures they took and the things they bought to reflect on years and years down the line would trigger memories from this trip. They would hand their Mission Beach Christmas ornament year after year, use the Pacific Coast Highway cups they paid way too much for, an Oceanside California oven mitt, a puzzle of a palm tree, and all of those things. Looking at those will give them a few minutes to remember their honeymoon and the great time they had as life continued to move forward when they are back home.

The next day was exactly what I had expected. Late in the morning, they began to pack up my back seat and trunk with all their belongings and shopping bag after shopping bag of all the things they bought on their trip. I could see a tiny bit of sadness as this was their last day. No more swimming in the ocean, no more exploring, no more souvenirs to buy.

It was unlike what I have known as traditional sadness, though. This was more of a feeling of a funk as the week went by so quickly and they had such a great time, not wanting it to end. But they were still grateful they had that time. With the car packed up and hotel keys turned in, they stopped before their departure and looked back at the beach.

"Just twelve hours ago, sitting on that bench after an amazing day. Listening to the ocean together, the wife said to the husband. "What an incredible week! I love you!"

The husband leaned over to kiss his wife and said, "I love you too."

With that, we were off. They had no plans on the way back for anything to add to their adventure. They just talked about getting back to see their dog, look at all the pictures they had taken, and start to get back to what they called "reality". They were still holding hands, the same as they did on the drive out. His right hand in her left. She would look down occasionally and smile at her new wedding ring. The sparkle that came off the one small diamond in it. They talked about their final full day the day before and recounted that they ate four times and stopped at eleven bars, having a drink at each one of them and taking a picture of themselves at every stop. Eleven bars, that sounds impressive. Probably better they did not drive the day before.

Crossing back over the Arizona state line, the wife turned down the radio and said, "I have an idea. Hear me out. How would you like to take a honeymoon every year?"

The husband looked on with a bit of confusion, but interest. "Explain," he said, with a humorous tone.

"Well, I'm not thinking of anyone else, just us. But think about how many people get too busy and absorbed with all the things that really do not matter much. Then they wonder where ten years went, and they haven't done much of anything fun. Or they become miserable and forget why they got married. I want, at a minimum, at least once a year to spend a week with you. No obligations other than just being together; shut everything else out. I want to go out and explore and see new things with you. Or go back to places we love and do that again. A time where it's just us. And we never miss a year of doing it."

The husband took in the proposal. "What if we have a really lean year, just one of those years where all sorts of things go wrong, and we're too tight on money?"

She paused to think of an answer. "We still go. We still get away from the house, get away from work, and go. We can go camping or get a real cheap motel out of Phoenix. That way, we spend an entire week together without the distractions of being at home. Just us."

He processed this more; and smiled. "I think it is a great plan, but what do you mean by a honeymoon each year? This just sounds like a vacation, which is still great, but you only get one honeymoon."

"Says who?" the wife responded back, giving him a playful delicate slap on the arm. That bitch. I learn sarcasm more and more as time goes by. "This is our marriage and our story. We do what we want. Call it a vacation, call it a honeymoon, but I say a honeymoon. Spend that week each year remembering why we married each other and that time always reconnecting when it is just us. Whatever label we put on it, it will always give us something to look forward to. Anything else will just be a vacation. What do you say?"

"This is a great idea!" he said while lifting his hand with hers in to kiss it. In a more serious tone, he asked her "What do we do if we have kids later on? How does that fit into this equation?"

Without missing a beat, she tells him, "Simple. They come along! Or they get a week at the grandparent's house if we go somewhere, I don't know…, more adult, if that makes sense. I think it would be great to have kids come with us. I don't want to build a life where something like this is not an option. I don't want us to be seventy years old wondering why we didn't celebrate this marriage as often as we could. Think about getting remarried in Las Vegas for the hell of it, or even if we say our "I do's" to each other in New York city, just the two of us. Some random place there. But a week for us, every year. A solid week."

He looked over at her, cracking a bit of a smile, only taking his eyes off the road for a second, and said "You remember what you said to me when I asked you to marry me last year?"

She smiled and said, "Yes! You caught me off guard!" They both laughed.

I could tell this was something I had not learned about them, as much as they talked about their lives together, I had never heard about the proposal. "I'm in," she said. "That is what I told you when you proposed. Not I do. Not yes. I'm in."

He said to her, "Well, I'll give you the same answer you gave me. I'm in!"

33

They both laughed and smiled at this.

The wife even said, "I guess we will be seeing you again next year, car!" as they would occasionally speak to me, typically to thank me for getting them to and from their destinations. Always giving me a delicate pat on the dashboard to thank me when saying it. And a smile. I have to say; I would be ecstatic to see these two again on honeymoon number two. Or any of their honeymoons. These two will make it and have one hell of a good journey in doing so.

5.

The Loan Roadtripper

I had hoped at least at some point, since I am a rental car, that I would be able to get out and see some of the country. I mean, really get out. More than what I saw on my train and trailer ride out to Arizona. Even the great jaunts I had a little outside of Arizona. No, I really wanted to experience this country; I wanted to stretch my tires, travel some long distances, and see some of these things I heard people talk about. Put some real miles on, let the wind blow through me, maybe even have the windows down. Away from the boring local business trips and pointless everyday destinations. There have already been some great times, but I wanted a true road trip. I want to see some changes in scenery; and go through a few different states. I really did not even care what time of year; I just wanted to do a real long drive. Just drive, and drive, and drive. This was one trip I was glad to take, and I was glad to take this guy on it. Probably one of the best trips in my entire experience as a rental car. I say that a lot. I know.

I was dropped off at a rental branch out in the suburbs the night before, away from the airport where I was usually rented out. This one was inside a grocery store. Quite the small branch, and somewhat odd. A real slow volume of people drifted in and out, with only one employee working. Rarely was I ever taken away from the airport.

I saw him come in on a Tuesday in the early afternoon. He seemed a little quiet at first. Just looked like a regular, average guy. Nothing really stood out about him. He presented his rental agreement to the employee. A one full week rental. They took a walk around with the company agent and inspected me. No huge scratches, no dents, no cracked glass. This was the standard operating procedure everybody went through. He signed the papers for a week's rental, and the rental agent handed him the keys.

My new driver said to him, "I'll take care of it." And he sure did.

I wasn't sure what the agenda was. He sat down, drove out of the grocery store strip mall, and headed to his home about a mile away. It did not look like much where he lived, simple basic condo. Nothing really stood out, kind of the same as his appearance. He made a few trips in and out of the house and packed me with what I would usually see a single guy have, not much baggage. It was winter, so he had an extra jacket and a larger backpack, and then he brought out something I had never see a single driver have for a short drive. A cooler. No one brings a cooler on a short drive. This was when I knew it was going to be a long trip. That long road trip I had wanted for such a long time. Where were we going, I wondered?

He got back into my driver's seat, turned on my ignition, turned up the heat, and shut the radio off. It was February and still quite cold outside. Enough where I could see frost on the bushes outside his home. That air that had an uncomfortable chill to it, especially when the wind blew. He opened a road atlas, something else I had not seen. Actually, it was something I had only heard about until then, and that was it. They did exist. Usually, it was someone looking at their phone and coming ungodly close to crashing me and killing themselves, more times than they would ever know looking at those damn things while driving. He was still quiet, slowly gazing over the atlas, just taking his time. It was much larger than an average book; and appeared to be brand new. It still had a price tag on the back cover.

He looked at each page for two or three minutes, slowly reviewing so many different locations. I could see him running his finger over highways, seemingly no real route, just scanning different parts of the country. His head never moved, but his eyes constantly shifted, following his finger as he traced imaginary routes on the pages. Everything was on this map. Interstates, country roads, rural routes, lakes, streams, mountains. Everything.

Usually, I knew where I was going; or had some sort of sense of it from people's phones or their conversations. Even hand-written instructions or something printed out to give me a general idea of the destination. Not this guy. He took his time looking over a few different pages of maps. Arizona, New Mexico, California, Utah, Colorado, Texas, and a lot of surrounding states. The question for me came up again, where were we going? He had no invitations, no address written down, nothing. He was quiet doing so. Somewhat methodical; but very quiet. I will never forget how initially silent he was. He never said a thing looking over that map.

There was a look of sadness that came from him. When he looked up from the map, I saw him look towards his home, almost like he was hesitating to depart. He even sighed, a real deep breath like he was thinking about not leaving. Now I was intrigued.

He had me booked for a week and I still had no idea where we were going. This really looked like he had prepped for a long drive, the cooler was a sign, and it was heavy. The suspense was killing me! Then I saw it; a tear came down his cheek. A slight sniffle followed. He quickly wiped at his cheeks and eyes and put the map down on my passenger seat just as fast as the tear came down. Then I thought I knew why, or at least started to get a suspicion looking at his left hand. Specifically, his left ring finger. A slight tan line around where I would see a wedding ring; it looked like it was recently removed. He hooked up his seatbelt, and backed me out of the parking space, and headed towards the highway, headed up north. We passed the Phoenix area and kept going up in elevation. Doesn't this guy know that it is snowing less than one hundred miles away? Why were we headed toward it? Why go up north in that?

He did not say anything, did not turn the radio on. Just silence, only the sounds of my motor running and the occasional shift from the transmission. Nothing from him. He had a sadness that I had not seen in anyone, and it seemed to linger like an awkward conversation. He was breathing heavy and slow still, sounding like he was trying to relax and calm down constantly. I really wished he would turn on the radio. Something. Anything. Then it changed; he started talking to me. Well, he was talking out loud, but little did he know that I was listening. Nobody knows I am listening. After the end of our week together, it seemed like that was all he needed. Just someone to listen to him.

It stated out, with just a few random words here and there, nothing that I could really put together. Then he said something that stuck with me. Something I was hoping I would hear or at least sense from him. Those seven words put me, and most importantly, him, at ease. "I am going to be all right."

Then his demeanor really changed, and something else happened that was more common than most people would think. He started talking to me. Directly to me. "Hey, car, I need to get out of my town for a while. I have absolutely no idea where I'm going, what I'm doing, and no plan on where I'm going to stay. No reservations. And I don't care at all. I've got you for a week and wherever I wind up, that'll be where we go. I'm just going to drive with no destination, no plan, and no agenda. There's no direction in my life, and because of this, I forgot how to be happy. Nothing to look forward to. I forgot how to smile. I'm going to take this week to change that, or at least try. You're in this with me!" He stopped himself, not with a laugh or a smile, but something that broke up the sadness. "Wherever we go, that'll be where we wind up. It could be awesome, or it could completely suck. This could be making a ton of memories or a week of coming back wondering why I wasted all this time and money I don't have right now. I have no idea. But we are doing it. I really think no plan on this journey is the best plan."

Rock. On.

We made our first stop a few hours north of Phoenix in the town of Flagstaff, Arizona. From what I gather, a pretty decent size college town in the mountains. Driving in, I saw him scanning the side of the road, looking for a motel. It was getting late, and the sun had set about an hour previously.

After driving about a half mile down the main street close to the downtown area, we saw the all too familiar neon sign with a flashing "vacancy" sign. I could see he was tired. This place has nothing special about it, just a standard motel that had about twenty-five units and all the parking in the front. No pool at all, an old paint job, and years of weather-beaten paint in the parking lot to barely indicate each parking stall. No perks, no amazing amenities. No gym to be seen. I would put any amount of money on it that there was no business center at this location either. This was the kind of place where all you cared about was four walls, a bed, and a ceiling. He pulled into the spot, just worn out and tired. Without missing a beat, he stepped into the front office and came out a few minutes later with a key. He only took one of his bags and the road atlas from the passenger seat. Without a word, he stepped into the room, and a few minutes later, the lights went out from the window. That is the end of this day.

The next morning, he stepped out of the room pretty early, just a few minutes after sunrise. He was wearing a fresh set of clothes and looked like he had just had a shower, his hair still wet. There was still some snow on the ground throughout the parking lot.

I watched him stand there for a few minutes, looking over the horizon and letting the crisp air hit his face. A bit of a smile appeared, if even for a brief moment. He closed his eyes and let the brisk wind hit his face. He briefly looked over to me, retreated back to his room, and grabbed the bag he had brought in for the night and the same road atlas. That gigantic road atlas. He got into the car; and placed it in the same location when we left, right on my passenger seat. Situating himself and getting the heat started in the car, then picked up the atlas again.

"Where to go, where to go, where to go?" he repeated, his finger running over the state of Arizona. The same thing he had done the day before, his fingers traced over routes of so many different places. He let out a sigh, "Do we want to see the ocean, or do we want to go somewhere we have never been before?" He contemplated these two options over and over for a while. Then, he pulled a coin from his pocket and said out loud, "Heads, we see the ocean. Tails, we head east." That familiar "ping" sound with a coin flip followed, he watched the silver color spin in the air and caught it in one hand, turning it over on the top of his other hand. He moved it over and revealed where we were going. I saw the eagle wings. Tails.

We were heading east.

This put us out on Interstate 40, headed to Albuquerque, New Mexico. Which I assumed was our destination. Who knew? This road did not have much to look at. At least in terms of major attractions. Just a desert landscape and occasional small towns here and there. I always wanted to see more of these small roadside towns that we were passing by. The tiny local shops selling trinkets of the area, usually painted in a color that really stood out from the brown landscape. Every so often, we passed by abandoned old buildings just off the interstate.

I noticed his smile started to come back more than yesterday. A little at a time. He took a moment every so often to look from the road out into the desert. We stopped every few hours, filled me back up with gas, and he would always go inside each store to get a drink and some sort of snack. But with every stop, we would not immediately get back on the road. He would take his time to enjoy his drink and whatever food he bought. Usually sitting on the hood of me and look out at what was in front of us. Just took his time, soaking in all the surroundings and snapping pictures of every stop. He just seemed to enjoy every stop we were at. Every time he did that and got back in the car, the smile would come back. He would pick that road atlas again, look over the destinations, options, and at what else was around he might want to go to.

As we continued east, we made a few more stops outside of gas stations. If a little tourist trap caught his attention, we would pull off the road and go in. Or buildings with brightly painted buildings we had seen over the last few hours. He would always write down inside that road atlas where he stopped and a quick note of what he saw and did there. We left Arizona and crossed into New Mexico, and the scenery changed. The colors around us went from more of that traditional brown desert we had been in all day to a red tint. This was what a road trip was all about. Sure, I had some long stretches driving, but nothing like this. It was great!

I called the location right! He pulled into Albuquerque in the early evening. A little off the Interstate, he drove in and headed towards downtown. "Where are we staying? Where are we staying?" he kept saying, always asking questions about our destination more than once. He scanned down a few streets looking for the familiar neon sign of "Vacancy" you see so often from the road. Just like the night before last, he found a place, much like the first one that fit his needs, a bland motel with a low per evening price advertised. With a faded paint job and potholes in the parking lot. Possible prostitutes looking for their John, patrolling the area. "Well, if they have a room, this is where we are at for the night."

And we did. Was not five-star accommodations, but it worked. Not like

I was going inside anyway. It was still being relatively early in the evening, and after taking his bags inside, he went out. A night on the town from what I could gather as he walked down the street and out of my view.

I sat there in his absence, just listening to a new town. This new city I had never been to before. This was so much different than Phoenix. Sure, the same sounds of cars driving by, dogs barking, people talking, all of that were the same, but it was still different. Different smells came from the restaurants, along with people I had never seen before walking down the street out for their own fun that night, whatever that was. I could hear a faint bleed of noise from a concert venue down the street, making it all the way over to me. Although I was not capable of doing this, as much as I could, I started to smile as well. This was a vacation for me, too. I wondered where my driver was at. What was he doing? Meeting new friends? Getting a quality meal that did not come from a gas station microwave, perhaps, as his diet so far had me a bit bothered? I truly hoped so. Or at least out having a good time.

About five hours later he came back. It had started to get much colder, as the sun had been down for a while. I figured he would have gone right into his room, into the heat it provided and a warm bed. Some comfort from the elements. To my surprise, he came back out a few minutes later with a six-pack of beer he had bought at the last stop before we checked into the motel. Yeah, I saw him purchase that earlier. No judgment on my behalf. Instead of the protection of that room, he did what he had been doing most of the day. He came out, sat on my hood, and stood out in this small part of the world before him. The "crunch" of opening a can of beer and his first sip off of that.

"You know what car," he said, taking another generous sip from of the can, "I had a great night! They sell one of the best slices of pizza I have ever had, right down the street. Great beer, too. I caught them right before happy hour ended. Hung out with a few locals and caught the end of the game with them on the TV. Good group of people. And I walked, just walked. Probably four or five miles around town."

He took another large sip from the can, bringing it all the way to empty, and collapsed the aluminum can. Pulled out a second beer from the bag, I heard that "crunch" again when it opened, and he took another bountiful sip off from it. "I just walked, car, I just walked. A new city I have never been before. You know there's a concert going on right down the block?" he asked me. Yeah, man, I heard it, ever so faintly I heard it too. But I'm not getting on him for that. "So many people, out tonight, enjoying their lives. There is so much cool art around here, right on the buildings. This is life, car. This is life. A new experience, a new set of memories. I'm glad I had the courage to do this. I needed this. To get out. Just to get out." He looked back down at his beer, took another sip from it, and smiled. He looked back up towards the street, and said to me "You know, this part of Albuquerque is actually some of Route 66. The original road that went from California to Illinois. And we are both here on it."

He never really took his eyes off the road and kept talking about his knowledge of it while speaking to me, the road I now know as a portion of Route 66. All the while, still taking sips from his beer, opening up another one and spouting off all sorts of trivia he knew offhand about the original Route 66 to me. At this time, I noticed that his words became a bit slurred and less clear as time went on. Have another one, friend.

He continued to spew facts about a lot of the things we passed earlier in the day. There was a lot I was learning about this stretch of road from him. I supposed anyone else seeing this would think he was crazy. Or extremely drunk. Maybe he was. I was not saying anything. Sitting outside at night, talking to a car and possibly violating some law about an open container of alcohol in public. I have seen so much worse, but he kept talking about all he saw on his walk downtown. The new things he never knew existed, really happy about his night. Then he became silent, looking up towards the road.

On the sidewalk, a couple, probably in their late twenties, close to his age, I assumed, dressed up a little bit as people would do for a date night, were slowly walking on the sidewalk from what I concluded was a night out on the town together. They were holding hands and laughing. Maybe they were at the concert? Maybe just coming from a movie? Maybe it was a date night they had been looking forward to all week?

My driver looked down at his can of beer and drank the rest of it. A smile spread across his face as he watched them walk by. "It looks like they really had fun tonight, don't you think, car?" With his smile still full, I did see his eyes start to water a bit. He took a deep breath and looked up at the sky. Too bright in town to see much of any stars, he glanced up at the view.

He said something that clarified a little about his situation and why we were on this trip. But it sounded like he needed to say it out loud. "You know, car, I miss her. I miss her so much." It was spoken very slowly and with so much emotion. Then there was silence as he continued to look up at the sky for a few more minutes, still doing his best to keep a smile on. Without saying anything else, he went into his room and shut the light off.

It started to snow not even five minutes later. Not heavy snow by any means, just a light dusting that falls so slow it almost feels like time is getting ready to stand still. The kind of snow that makes everything else feel silent. A perfect end to the day.

The next morning, we headed north, eventually peeling off from the interstate. Northern New Mexico in this area was particularly flat. That never really changed much either, as we hit the panhandle of Oklahoma and even found our way into the bottom western portion of Kansas. The radio was on this time and the windows were cracked open a bit, letting in some air.

He did not speak much on this part, but he was looking out at everything before him. The large farms, huge bales of hay, and fields of cows. Even when we made it all the way to Kansas, he stopped to fill up on gas and went back to that comfortable spot of sitting on the hood. He ate a hot dog and sipped from a bottle of soda. Just looking out at the small town we were in.

Jumping back in, we headed back on the same route we had come from. He never said it, but I think we made our way to Kansas simply because it was just there. Another new place to go see and more miles to drive. When we headed back south, a particular part of Oklahoma on that day was a sight to be seen. We had been driving all day, only stopping for gas and small breaks. We were up at the top of Oklahoma, from what I saw on the road atlas, looked to be that little sliver of the state by Kansas and Texas. Not a very well-traveled road as other traffic only passed by every few miles. He had the radio on pretty low and seemed to be just reflecting on the day's drive; he was still talking to me about where we had been and what we had seen. Even though I was there with him, it brought comfort hearing him talk. I liked his voice.

Every so often, he would sing along to the radio, clearly with little knowledge of the complete lyrics of the songs being played. What he did not know he made up words with little thought to creativity or just started humming along. So many people do that. It was a break from the road noise; as terrible of a singer as he was, I welcomed it.

As we were heading southwest through this little part of the state on the way to Texas was when our view changed. It was completely dark in the east, and we could still see the sun and make out the landscape in the west. The land was so flat we could literally see night and day. It was something so amazing to be seen. Some stars in the east were starting to become visible. It was that perfect time of day that gave us this view. When he noticed it, he turned the radio off and just sat there driving and describing to himself what he was seeing. Complete darkness to the left and day to the right. Another pure sight of something truly beautiful on this drive. If I required breathing, this sight would have taken my breath away. He would only say one word for a while to describe what we were seeing, and it summed it up perfectly.

"Wow."

We pulled into a gas station later in a small town in North Texas that night. It seemed like the kind of place where everybody knew everybody. One grocery store, one gas station, and a lot of history. We pulled into the dirt lot in the front of one of the gas pumps, as we had done many times so far on this trip. That familiar sound of gravel crunched under my tires driving up. He got out, started filling my tank, and stepped inside the store, coming back shortly after with a bottle of soda and a bag of chips. His diet did not change once throughout this entire trip, nothing but junk food. Complete garbage. It was his trip, who was I to take that away from him? After filling up the tank, I saw him looking at the other side of the gas station, where stadium lights and a crowd noise were coming from the east of the building. He got back in, drove to the other side of the building, and we saw the source, just a small-town baseball game.

It had the representation of any game I would expect in this town. Twenty rows or so of bleachers, parents, friends, and classmates cheering on their team. Not a single empty seat was to be found. It appeared to be a high school game, and by the look of the small scoreboard well-lit from the stadium lights, we could see that the home team was up by 2 runs in the 5th inning. The smell of cheap overpriced hotdogs and fresh popcorn filled the air, mixed with freshly cut grass from the field.

A sound was made, that crisp-defined crack of a bat and ball making contact, and the cheers from the crowd immediately after that happens. Fans were all sporting their team jerseys and face paint. This was a true love of the game from this town. My driver got out and walked up to the fence just to see more clearly. Then the same gaze came over him I saw when he was truly enjoying himself again. That smile broke that he probably had no idea came through when he was just embracing the moment. It was there. Again. He was just enjoying being in the moment. I liked seeing that. Something as simple as a hometown baseball game that he had no stake in bringing even a bit more joy back into his life.

He just stood there by the fence, close to third base but away from other spectators. It did not seem to matter. He fit in as everybody did, just watching a game. Cheering for the home team he knew nothing about and clapping at every good play they demonstrated. As the game ended, he made his way back to me, turned on my ignition, turned off my radio, and just sat there in silence.

Still with the same crack of a smile, he said "What a good end to a game. I've always wanted to see a small-town game and never made any effort at home. I always wondered what an experience like that would be. Something so small to the world, but just to experience that. Gives me a little bit of an idea of what it would be like to live in a town like this. I think I'm better for it."

The next morning, we woke up in a similar lodging situation he had throughout the entire trip. An economical motel off a major highway with no distinguishing features. It seemed like he slept in a little more as the sun had already been up for over an hour before I saw the light of his room turn on. Half an hour or so later, he emerged from his room, bags in hand, and our morning started as the other ones had. Turning me on to get my heater started, and he pulled out that huge road atlas. I enjoyed seeing him do this, looking to see what the day's options were going to look like as he moved his finger along red and blue lines defining the routes available, still never moving his head, just scanning with his eyes. I liked seeing the notes he continued to write inside the road atlas, small details of where he stopped and what he did on the trip.

At this time, we had already driven a full day from Oklahoma the day before through Texas and found ourselves in Southeast New Mexico today. It was a long day of driving yesterday and enjoying the journey. We just took our time, viewing at all the options in the small towns we passed by. Seeing oil drilling equipment, Mom and Pop furniture stores, local bars and restaurants, and small-town schools. We soaked in the sights and saw what that part of the world had to offer. Stopped in every local museum and snapped pictures of all the sights along the way.

That day seemed like we were going to head back home or at least back west. When he was looked over the road atlas, he kept saying out loud, "Home or the ocean, home or the ocean? Or Las Vegas, maybe? Too cold to go to the Grand Canyon. Think we could make it out to San Francisco and back before I have to turn you in? I guess we'll figure it out tomorrow morning." It kept the theme of the trip alive, finding out where we wanted to go that morning and not thinking of it the day before. I loved it. I loved the thrill of it. That night we pulled into a cheap no-name motel off the side if the interstate again. He looked tired from the drive that day. There were a lot of miles driven today. Some good miles.

The next morning, he came out and pulled the cooler out to abuse the free ice machine just outside the motel office. I did not realize until then, but he hardly ever dug into that throughout the entire trip. He bought a lot of what he needed at gas stations along the way to take some time to just look out at the road he came from and what was in front of him.

It had been cold this entire trip; it was by far the most amount of snow I had ever seen before. Even the ice in the cooler that morning had not fully melted. But why turn down a chance to fill it with fresh ice? Even if it is so cold it will probably not melt. Like he said the night before, we still had no idea where we were going. There were still two more nights on my reservation, and many ideas were thrown out. After setting the cooler into the rear seat, he jumped back in and turned on my engine, getting my heat started. He blew into his hands to warm them up and picked up the road atlas again.

Ever the silent one, he looked that over, his head rarely moved and his eyes gazed at all the options we could drive to, still tracing routes with his fingers. Being so close to Arizona, I saw him moving back to look at the full state, looking north, looking all the way west as we would head towards California and hit the beach.

"Hhhhmmmmm" he said while moving his finger down south, reading out loud all the towns close to the border of Mexico. "I've got an idea, car. How about we go to a mining town?" It was almost like he was asking me for permission.

I wanted to tell him I was at his mercy; where he pointed my wheel would be where I go. Plus, it was something new I had still never seen.

We headed west and very soon after we started, we were back in the state of Arizona. Back to his home state. And according to my license plate, my home state as well. We took the path south off the interstate on a gorgeous drive, the one where the tan of the desert and the blue sky met as far as the eyes, or in my case, headlights could see, was miles and miles of this desert landscape. Hardly a cloud in the sky at that time. Just a huge blue sky. This was clearly not a well-traveled road by the lack of cars absent from the roads. We had seen this before. It was just the two of us. It felt good. It was so much fun to start a new adventure this day together.

After some time, we found ourselves pulling into the town of Bisbee, Arizona. He was right, an old quiet mining town. It had a charm to it that I had not seen before, with steep hills and brightly colored homes and businesses. It was old and historical but well kept up. Old bricks lined a lot of the streets and being still relatively early in the morning; businesses were slowly starting to open. Local shops and restaurants were turning their doors open for customers. The smell of a deep, rich coffee wafted from the café.

He parked on what I would consider the main drag of the town. He got out, looked up at the buildings down the street and took a short walk to grab breakfast and a coffee at a restaurant on the patio, just sat and watched this town start to get the day going. Smiling all the while.

He got back in, and took a quick drive around the town, exploring and driving up and down the narrow, steep hills of this town. He pointed out to me the small houses and wonder out loud how they could be built like that on such steep hills. He stopped inside a small shop and got himself another bottle of soda for the next leg of the trip. I really wished he would start drinking more water. As much fun as we are having, I wished he would get proper hydration.

We headed out of town after that and started to head up north. We passed through another place that went by the name of Tombstone, Arizona, where he stopped again to walk the town.

This place held the namesake well, with dirt-lined streets, and an old-west feel. Half of the people walking around wore duster coats and cowboy hats. Guns were fucking everywhere, yet everybody greeting each other in a friendly manner. There was actually a horse tied up to a post next to a local bar.

He took a few hours there, walking up and down the main drag of the town. I saw him every so often, exploring all the shops and talking with people. Once, I even saw him walking on the wood panel planks outside of all the shops with a huge ice cream cone. He even stopped inside a business that let you dress up like a cowboy and get your picture taken. Yeah, he did that too. For a brief period of time, he was a cowboy. After a couple of hours, he had his fill, and we were back on the road headed north.

In the early afternoon, we found ourselves driving through Tucson, Arizona. I could tell he did not want to stop there by his excessive speed over the legal limit and a few grumblings about how he was never a fan of that city. But I did see him look up at billboards the last few miles that kept advertising an old cowboy town, famous for filming old west movies and what they claimed to be a true piece of Arizona history. Cheesy billboards with cartoon cowboys, smiling cactus characters, and dancing horses. Christ. Between looking at the billboards and the clock, I could only imagine that he was calculating if he had enough time to explore that point of interest with adequate time before it was too late.

"You know what, car, I want to go see it. I went there when I was a kid a few times and want to see it again." And that was it, we headed west off the interstate, and a few miles later, we pulled into the attraction.

The parking lot was largely empty and still cold. It was quite windy. We pulled into a spot with a small patch of snow, and when he got out had to put on his jacket immediately. This was a true old west town as I actually saw a tumbleweed blow through the dirt in front of the building. Maybe that was his sign to go in the last couple of hours they were open. The tumbleweed.

He seemed excited, maybe it was to go back and re-live a place he was at when he was young, or maybe it was in the spirit of this trip he was on to experience as much as he could. He went in and came out a few hours later, with probably the biggest smile I had seen on him the entire trip yet. He came back into my driver's seat and opened up a bag of all sorts of trinkets he had bought. A t-shirt, shot glass, magnet, bar towel, and a hat. All sorts of shit.

He put the new hat on and looked at himself in the rear-view mirror with a big smile showing. He was happy. He went on for maybe a minute, telling me of all he did in the few hours before they closed, including riding a horse for thirty minutes, watching a gun fight show outside, taking a quick mine tour, and seeing a few places that he was able to recall where some his favorite movies were filmed. Maybe this brought him back to feeling like a little kid again, being back where he spent some time with his family. Then he did something that he had never done on the entire trip. Something I had hoped he would not do, but on a long enough timeline, I knew it would happen.

He made a decision.

He got out of me again and shut my door, leaning against my hood, watching the last few minutes of the sun before it fell under the horizon, bringing the night on. He just sat there and watched it, and took several deep breaths, relaxing. Just enjoying the view. The other patrons of the western theme park were all gone, leaving him alone in the parking lot. Even the employees had left at this point.

There were just the two of us.

In the fading light, something caught his eye. A movement just to the side of the entrance of the parking lot. A coyote. It just walked into distance and took a few steps into the parking lot and made eye contact with my driver. In was in no way an aggressive manner, just an animal doing what it does, and him looking back at the coyote with a smile. The coyote surveyed back at him for a few seconds and looked back at the landscape it came from. The animal at that time, much resembling the actions of the guy who rented me, seemed to be wondering, "Where do I go?"

The guy who rented me said in a calm and soft tone "Hey, coyote!" As quick as the coyote showed up, it slowly walked back into the now-dark desert. They briefly made eye contact, almost like an exchange letting each other know they meant no harm. Just going about their day.

After this interaction, he seemed to solidify a decision for the first time. He got back into my driver's seat, turned on my ignition to get the heat going, and said to me, "You know what car… I, I think we're done. I got what I needed out of this. We have more time, but I'll go home a day early. I saw what I needed to see, I did what I needed to do, and I felt how I wanted to. Feel even better than I thought I would. I'm just, well, going to go home. Home."

With that being said, we started the two-hour journey back to his house. Nothing else was said by him on that drive back. Not one word. He never even turned the radio on again. I did not think he had to. I think he was reflecting on all that he had seen and done the last few days and how he felt better. He conquered whatever he was dealing with at that time. Sometimes the view of the road and the time to think about whatever one needs to can answer a lot of questions. Where that was all one needed to do to make sense of what I have heard people call life.

Well, that was it. Quite a journey. This guy was smiling a lot more now. He was changed. Hell, I felt changed from his experience. I was so happy at first just knowing I was going to see more of the country, but it made it so much better realizing that I was a catalyst that helped this guy get through a tough point in his life. Being a car and all. I knew it sounded strange, but I thought I felt better that this guy was better. He pulled back into his home, the same spot we started from. Around twenty-five hundred miles together almost a week ago. Twenty-five hundred rewarding miles. Miles on a car meant I had aged more, but the experience was worth it.

He got out and walked up to the front door of his place, coming back a few more trips to gather the rest of his things. I knew I would really miss that guy, the thrill of not knowing where we were going that day and what we would see. His last trip back to the car was one of the first things he brought in, that huge road atlas. It had more pen marks in it, a few more creases, and dents in the cover. The coffee spill all over the map of New Mexico, and the spine no longer had the crisp sound when it opened, but it had a story. All the notes he wrote in it. Just like me, just like him. A new story. He picked it up and shut my passenger door, where that atlas sat for the last week on the seat. I felt it was almost a third companion on this expedition.

Admittingly, I had to say I will miss that atlas as well. While it never dictated where we went, it helped get us to our destinations, wherever they would be that day. It was the first time I had ever seen one. Maybe the last. It helped me feel like we took a bit of a trip in the past, where people navigated with maps instead of technology telling them where to go like a mindless drone. It added to the true road trip experience.

Once all of his things were taken out, and we were back to where we started from, parked in the same spot outside of the condo, he came back out, opened a can of beer, and leaned up against my passenger side door. He still had that smile on his face when he really started to enjoy himself and the journey. He even looked back at me, with a slight laugh realizing that he had been talking to a car for almost a full week. It was all good, my friend. All good. He looked up at the sky for a few minutes, just watching the few stars you could see in the Phoenix metro area. He said quietly, "Wherever she is, I hope she is OK. I still miss her. I still miss you."

It was at that time, I realized I had never really learned what had happened to him beforehand. What was he going through that he needed to take this trip? I never learned who "She" was that he referred to. At the end of it, I supposed it really did not matter whether I knew or not. He got something out of our experience together that seemed to help him, and that was all that really mattered.

He took one more picture of himself smiling with me next to him, making sure I was in the shot. The final picture of his trip. A picture I had hoped would have been taken of me from a new owner at the dealership as a brand-new car. The look of pride that came with those types of pictures. He took a ton of photos on this journey, and in this last one, he really, really looked happy. A completely changed person. I knew he would drop me off tomorrow morning, but that was all business. Tonight was the best time to say our good-byes.

I still think of him often and our trip together, and I hope he is still doing well and continues to find his journey and happiness.

6.

The Last Goodbye

I hoped I would never be a part of this or even see it, but due to the nature of being a rental car, I saw different situations all the time. I suppose it was inevitable, and it did happen.

She came to the rental car lot and had a sad, sad look on her face. I really could not make out much about her destination and what was happening. She just looked sad. She said nothing as she climbed into my driver's seat. Nothing in the hour or so drive we had, heading south of the Phoenix area. No radio on. Nothing.

Just sadness.

We drove down to a place between Phoenix and Tucson, Arizona. Not much in the town, we pulled off into the parking lot that had a gas station with a fast-food place attached. It seemed more like a stop off for truck drivers and people on a road trip to gas up, get something to eat, and get back on the road. People seemed to hurry through these places. It always seemed common in small towns along the interstate. A town with a name one would forget as soon as they heard it; they would not remember it as soon as they passed by it. Once parked, she sat in my driver's seat for only a minute, but from what I could tell for her, it seemed like an eternity. She was tense and I could feel it. She wiped a few tears from her eyes and got out of the car. No, this was different. I was sure she was not on a fun trip.

She stood outside when we arrived, looking attentively towards the road she came in on. The sun had gone down on our drive. Only the fading light from the west was apparent, still giving some light and the sunset that was always so beautiful in Arizona. She was so focused on the road she came in on she did not seem to notice. She did not seem to really notice anything, and she never took her eyes off the road for even a second, just leaning up against me on my driver-side door. There was a look of desperation on her face that I rarely saw in people. It was like whatever she was waiting for was all that mattered to her.

Then I saw a change in her face; she put on a smile as best as she could and gave a wave to a car coming towards us. I always loved seeing people wave. I loved seeing people smile. It meant they were happy. From her, it seemed forced, but as the car she was waiting for pulled up, she walked up to their passenger side, gave a bigger smile, and she had no more tears. When I saw the passenger door start to open, I understood why.

The driver of the other car got out and came to the passenger side, he gave a hug to the lady that drove me up and then opened the passenger door. The two of them helped a younger lady out from the passenger side. She seemed to be a similar age to the other driver, maybe twenty or twenty-five years younger than the lady who drove me up there.

Then it all made sense when I saw the new woman get out. They looked so similar, it was clear she was my driver's daughter, but she did not look well. She was sick. I could tell the second she came out of the car, assisted by her mother and who had to be her daughter's husband. She looked very frail; her skin was a color I had never seen before. They both smiled slightly as they helped her out of the car, and her daughter did the best she could to move a tube that was hooked up to her arm to the side so she could embrace her mother in a hug so genuine I had no words to describe it. None. Pure love. They stood there, assisted by leaning up on her mother and just held each other. Both started to cry softly but her mother got ahold of herself faster and said so calmly and softly next to her head, "I love you so much, my beautiful, precious child. My baby."

The daughter held on to her mom tighter and said, "I love you so much. You are the best mom in the world."

Her mom said, a little quieter, a little slower, "You are the best part of my life."

The husband, who drove them up looked over at his mother-in-law, smiled at her, and started to walk towards the store, leaving them alone to be together. To give them their time. I looked at the two left, the mother and daughter, still holding each other's hands and looking right at each other. Both were doing their best to give a smile.

I listened as the daughter told her mother in detail that her sickness had spread and the worst they feared was coming true. The little bit of hope they had left was gone. She told her mother that this was it. She was going to die. She clung to her mom tightly, and all they said to each other was, "I love you." I did not know how many times they said it, but the more I learn, I knew that no person ever gets tired or will get tired of hearing that. Just saying, "I love you."

She told her mother that she might only have one or two days left to live and wanted to spend it by going back to see the house she grew up in before the family moved away a few years ago, just outside of Phoenix. They were going to drive by her old high school where she was a member of the theater she loved so much, go by the restaurant she had her first job at and get one more slice of pizza from there, if she could eat. They talked so much about how they loved that place and how proud her mother was of her coming in to see her working at her first job. She was going to have her husband drive her up to north Arizona, around Payson, where they spent time together as a family growing up and the same place they were married just a few years before.

She said once they were there, her husband was going to ask to re-marry her, with just the two of them, even if it only lasted a day, a couple of hours, or a few minutes, because with her, a few more minutes to let her know how much he loved her meant the world to both of them. Then she talked about the last place they were going to on their trip, where she went up with her friends as a teenager to get out of the heat of Phoenix in the summer, Forest Lakes, where she used to hike, around the lakes in the area as best as she could and lay out on the grass by the water. Just to sit there and close her eyes and truly be at peace before death; at the same as the place gave her so much happiness in life. The place where she could smell the lake water blowing from the wind on to her face. The place where she would sit and listen to families laughing together, parents teaching their children to fish and hearing them all cheer in excitement when someone had their first catch.

At this time of year, the wildflowers were in bloom, and they talked about how much they would love to see them gently sway with the wind. Like the flowers were waving to them. She wanted her last moments to be up at a place that meant so much to her, just to lay out on the natural grass, feel the wind come through the pine trees, listen to the sounds, and smell the pine needles of those trees one more time, all of which was something she always treasured. It was something she called her soundtrack to a great life. The place she always considered to be her church. She wanted to smile and remember everything that place had meant to her, look back on all the great things she had done and the people in her life at such a young age. Then she wanted to go to sleep just one more time. That would be her last trip.

She looked up at her mom and said, "Hey, do you remember the one day when we woke up early on a Saturday? You really wanted to get out of town, so we drove up north by the lake where we saw the huge field of flowers, and I ran into them, making a trail behind me?" The Mom nodded. "Mom, I was so happy that day! It was just the two of us and you smiled so much looking at me in that field. How old was I then? What, eight? Nine?"

Her mom said, "I will never forget that. I'll remember that look on your face every time I think of you. You were so happy and so full of joy. That huge smile you have always had. Do you remember when you picked some flowers and put them in my hair?"

"I can't believe you remember that!" the daughter exclaimed, laughing.

Her mom did the best she could, but I saw a tear fall. "I remember that. I think about that memory each day. I've never forgotten about it."

Her mother told her one more time, hesitated, took a deep breath, and said "I will be there with you on the last day. If you want me to."

"No, I want you to remember this." Then she smiled at her mother, the same one she had given to her throughout her life. "Remember our time before today, even when I got sick. I know you so well that you can't go through anymore and see me like this. My husband will be there. He has loved me as much as you have, and you know that. You've done your job, and you did it better than anyone else could have. There's nothing I can tell you to really let you know this, mom, but you did it right. I was the most loved daughter in the world. You gave me a magical Christmas every year. You were at every theater performance, planned all my birthday parties, made me all my meals, took me on weekend road trips in the state, and loved me. Every single day. We had our time, and it was the best! I want to spend my last moments with just me and my husband."

Her mother nodded again, clearly understanding what she wanted, and knew it was time. It was time for them to go. Her husband returned and stood off to the side, trying not to be noticed, just giving them time. All three of them knew that the precious little time they had left was ticking. Fast.

She leaned in once more, gave her mother the biggest hug, and said to her, "If you ever want to see me, go to the pine trees up north. Lay down in the grass as I did so many times and close your eyes. Take a deep breath. Smile. Always smile. I got my smile from you. My smile that you love so much! Keep your eyes closed and keep smiling. Soon after, you will hear the wind through the trees; then you will feel the wind hit you. I want you to know that wind will be me, giving you another hug. It may not be the face you know, but it will be me. You can come to me anytime, mom. Just talk to me when you are up there. When you feel the wind, just talk to me. I will hear you. I will always be there for you as you were always there for me my whole life. I want you to keep riding your bike by the canal, I want you to keep fostering dogs, I want you to keep going down to that bar near your house to sing karaoke, I want you to keep volunteering, I want you to live your life. Go talk to that guy that you have a crush on. He has one on you. I see it every time we went there. Just know that I lived more in the years that I had than most people do five times my age. I lived every day. Every single day. I want you to do the same. We will see each other again, but not for a long time, and we will pick back up where we left off at then. I will tell Grandma that you said hello, and I am certain when I see her with the same big smile she always had. I may be gone, but I will never leave you mom. I love you."

Her mother gave her a kiss on the forehead. Her daughter took off the scarf she had around her neck, placed it around her mother's neck, and turned away to back to her car. The one I learned that she gave to her daughter the day she started middle school. The same scarf she wore as often as she could because she loved it so much. Her husband helped her into the car, and I watched as her mother did her best to stand there as strong as she could while the car started, and the two of them backed out. The daughter looked back at her mother, gave a last smile and a wave, which her mother mirrored.

She rolled down the window and heard her mother say, "I love you so much, my girl!"

Her daughter, using energy she did not have leaned out the car's window smiling and said, "I love you, mom. I love you so much. Good-bye." They turned out of the parking lot and drove away.

Her mother took a red handkerchief out of her pocket and started to wave it in her hand, the same she always did anytime her daughter drove away, either leaving for work, for school, to hang out with friends. I had learned through their conversation that it was the way her mother always was able to say "I love you" one more time when they could not hear it but see it from the rear-view mirror. The handkerchief was enough when her daughter looked back, it was the last part of the wave her mom gave to her that she could see. She watched as the two of them drove away, never breaking contact, watching the car drive away until it got on the interstate and went far enough into the distance that she could not see the lights from it any longer.

That was the last time she would ever see her daughter. That was it. She opened my driver's seat door, climbed in, and started crying. She took both of her hands up and clung to the scarf her daughter put around her neck and put it up to her face, just to smell her daughter again. A purple scarf. She wiped some of her tears with it and just continued to break-down crying.

If I could trade spots with her daughter so they could have just one more day together, I would.

7.

The Inadequate Bottle

There is an overwhelming abundance of restroom facilities throughout the United States and while they may not be in the best of sanitary conditions, they would get the job done. Life will go on. You foolish mortals have no idea how blessed you are. This guy missed the memo.

Another average guy, an average rental agreement, a couple days rental. I figure this would be a standard situation. Nope. Nope. Nope. While people who rent me sign a rental agreement that animals are not allowed in the car, that would have been a more fitting situation. Most pets I know were at least housebroken. They may leave some hair on the seats and dogs seemed to drool a bit, never wipe their feet off, sure, whatever. No ill intentions from them. Nothing I could not handle. I liked dogs. This is getting ahead of itself; I do not want to spoil the "magic" on this road trip to hell.

He rolled down the window right out of the rental lot, and the weather was awesome. Perfect temperature at that time of year. Not too hot, not too cold. I was all in favor of it. Gets a little air in me, blew out some dead skin cells, took a bit of smell out of me, made me a bit "younger", at least by the standards of a car. Similar to what humans would call a bath. It is amazing how fast you can age as a car with so many different butts in the seats.

It was one of those days when you just really wanted to be outside. It started out great. I emphasize, started out. He had his phone displayed, looking at the directions of where he was going. It seemed to be a couple of hours' drive outside of Phoenix. At this time of year, I loved being out, and I understood why people live here in the desert in the winter. If I had eyes, I would close them and just enjoy being in the moment on the highway with a new adventure at heart, hands spread open, just enjoying the moment.

What I didn't know as this trip would unfold was that the adventure would turn into a complete outright and utter Goddamn nightmare.

He pulled off to get provisions; what I continued to learn was what people called gas, snacks, and drinks. Sometimes lottery tickets that never, ever win. He was at the gas pump, filled the tank, and then ventured into the store for what was not available outside. Not a large man, yet he returned with what I would consider many items for a person of his stature. A sixty-four-ounce fountain beverage, four bottles of water, two cans of an energy drink with a wrestler on the side of the can I could only assume had already been dead for over a decade, and this other abomination of a food source I have heard people call "beef jerky." Apparently, it was subsistence for people that resembled some sort of hopelessness meal of meat, salt, and dehydration. How could that be healthy? He bought a lot of that shit. Bags of it.

The trip continued as many others do. Being by himself, he was relatively quiet, scanning over the radio for music he liked. Even caught the last part of some sports ball game on the radio that I would never understand. An occasional burp and fart from him. Then came what I have less than affectionately called "the move". The all too familiar motion with this I saw most people do when they have had a lot to drink and had not stopped for a while. The constant shifting around in the seat, scratching of genitals, and turning the radio down as if that would help. This guy needed to use the bathroom. One mile away, I saw a turn off, multiple opportunities for himself to take care of business. Nope. He kept going. Eight miles down the highway was another exit with not only one but six fast-food restaurants. Six. I think I even saw an unmarked buffet restaurant. Gas stations. Hell, there was even a halfway decent hotel chain right off the highway. There were options. Good ones.

The opportunity presented itself. He turned a blind eye.

Eventually, we passed a sign that said: Next services 48 miles.

While I do not like to ruin a story, here is the spoiler alert. We did not make it those forty-eight miles. The next ten minutes of my life were ones I would like to scrub out, but in true rental car fashion, if there was no visible damage, then I guess it never really happened, right? I supposed I would be happy that this guy saved one of his empty water bottles for the inevitable makeshift toilet he decided to fashion on the spot then and there instead of completely relieving himself directly on my floor. It had happened before. Humans seemed to view themselves as sophisticated and refined, putting themselves above most other living things on the planet. Still, they had no problem literally shitting where they ate. This guy had me questioning how humans made it to the top of the evolutionary chain.

I knew what was going to happen before it did. He opened up the cap to the empty water bottle and then formed an "invisible" seat. I was aware of horror stories about this, but it was something that you would think would never happen to you. Like "I do not need a car alarm; no one will ever break into my car", then months later, they come out to find the window smashed and the stereo missing. The invisible seat meant he was fashioning his hips higher up enough to let human biology and gravity happen as it does with what I can only determine as basic hydraulics.

With perfect execution, this maneuver was a well-balanced symphony of my driver, with one hand on the wheel, the other on his, well, penis, and then elevated slightly above the empty water bottle, where he could drain his bladder into a receptacle that can be capped and discarded at an appropriate waste removal point. I would give him this; the initial set up was completely by the book. He even kept full eye contact on the road and nodded at another motorist on the opposite side of the highway that would have never seen him or cared anyway, just to "keep up appearances," as I saw people do when they were trying to get away with something they should not.

That was what happened in this situation. He was trying to get away with something he should not have done. While this execution seemed to have the intended results as it started out with success, there was one major factor that he did not put into this equation. That was the amount of what he drank previously, the size of the empty water bottle, and his ability to control the release of this liquid waste once the process started. Check all three of those items as a complete failure.

This guy really should have known something was wrong when parts of him started to become warm and wet, but due to the invisible "booster chair" he created for himself, he was pissing on my floor, the seat, and once it was beyond the point of a remedy for the situation, his own hand. He filled up the water bottle and kept going. If I have learned anything about humans was that with as much as control they have over things, bodily functions are not one where sole ownership was controlled. Preservation to remove waste seemed to have a way of taking over a judgment call to cease and desist when the process had already started. When overwhelmed in this type of situation, the control humans have over this seemed to decrease rapidly. This was a prime example.

Once he realizes the error in his plan, he becomes panicked and loses what little control he has left. "Ah, Shit!" was what I heard before he became unglued at the situation. Fight or flight took over, and the pressure from the urine increased rapidly as he realized this was the point of no return. It had gone from a "controlled burn" with urine being contained to only the floor and seat to a complete disconnect. Pressure increased with the stress of the situation, and he began pissing on my steering wheel, instrument cluster, and in a last-minute attempt to preserve any sort of control over the situation, he tried to "aim" out of my window. At this point, the music was fading, along with the pressure of the release, which just had him pissing on the inside of my door panel.

Fuck.

In the chaos of the situation, he still never took his eyes off the road. I will give him that. Because safety first, right?

8.

Notable Quotes and Situations

It may be important to note that not all people who have rented me have some sort of epic story or life-changing situation come out of it. My time with them did not stand out in any major way. Most of the time, that was usually my experience. I was there to serve a basic transportation need, and it was as simple as that. It might be a little bit of a break with some of the ones that actually did stand out. However, some of them said or did one thing that was stupid, insulting, made me laugh, or weep for the human population. Typically, these were a one liner with words vomited out with no thought beforehand of how it would sound or something I saw that completely boggled my mind.

There following are some of the said quotes and my thoughts immediately afterward. The situations were just, well, kind of the same thing.

QUOTES:

"There is absolutely no way I am going to score any pussy with this car over the weekend."

-Well, not with that attitude.

Guy was out on a first date. He picked up a girl completely out of his league and told her, "Yeah, this is the car I'm driving now. Wanted something economical because my sports car isn't eco-friendly. Just doing my part to make a difference!"

-Dude, I saw that shitbox sedan in your driveway. You did not have any money. Sports car, my ass. Runaway girl, run away.

"God, I hate rental cars."

-Well, I am not all that fond of you either. Yet here we are. Why the hell did you rent one, then? No horse and buggy available today?

A guy had trouble explaining the eighteen-inch scratch on the front bumper to the rental car lot attendant, "No, that scratch was there before I picked up the car."

-Really? You sure you did not find it on the light pole you ran into last night? Asshole.

"All weekend in Las Vegas and I couldn't get laid once."

-Not every hunt is successful. Including the beaver hunt, sir.

"This is only what $39.99 a day gets me?"

-Sorry, I am not a supercar, but you are more than welcome to buy the one across town if my needs do not fit yours. You also paid for an economy and got a mid-size. Be happy.

"This car is ugly as hell."

-Look in the rearview mirror. Feeling is mutual, pal. Your haircut sucks.

"No, I cannot eat there; it's against my diet. How about we go across the street and get a double bacon cheeseburger?"

-What the hell kind of diet are you on?

"This car is a piece of shit."

-Christ, I just do not have the energy for this one today.

"I don't like this car. I just do not like this car. It is uncomfortable and boring. I just don't like this car. So boring."

-It is a twenty-four-hour rental; do you think you will be all right? Should we call someone?

"This car sucks. I should just turn it in early and end this vacation sooner."

-Well, that certainly would be the most expedient thing to do.

SITUATIONS:

It may not be something a person said, but more of what they did that stood out and made me think, "What?" These were the situations.

I watched a guy eat an entire large pizza from his lap while driving in rush hour traffic, only stopping to wipe the grease off his hands onto the seat. Thanks.

Swapped out and stole my almost new car battery for your old one. Really? You paid sixty bucks for a one-day rental just to do this? With gas and time, would it not just be as easy to buy a new battery?

Random guy in my passenger seat rolled my window down, then up, then down, then up, etc. For a while. When the window went down, he said, "Window down." When the window went up, he said, "Window up." This went on for seventeen minutes. Seventeen minutes.

A lady who rented me realized she forgot her make-up mirror and ripped off the one from my passenger seat visor and put it in her purse. All the make-up in the world was not going to work for her anyway, but at least she got some hope from it.

One guy found ten to twelve potato chips spilled in the back under my passenger seat that were not found by the cleaning "professionals" in between rentals. He ate all of them. They had been there for three weeks. Floor chips. If I could puke, that would have happened.

A lady came out of a fast-food restaurant with no food. Only fifty-eight ketchup packets that she consumed on her ride. She bit the side of them open and sucked the contents out. Want to know how I was aware there were fifty-eight of them, exactly? She left the empty packets on my passenger floor. Beautiful.

Two guys drank an entire bottle of vodka on a one-and-a-half-hour drive. The entire bottle. My driver had most of it. How were they still alive?

Gentleman driving alone who farted every five minutes and never rolled my windows down. Just breathed deeply, inhaling his own aroma. I had no way to understand the logic and appeal of this action. It was far from anything I enjoyed.

There was another gentleman driving with his family who farted, violently, every five minutes and never rolled the windows down. He breathed deeply, inhaling his own aroma. Rest of the family never said one word about this. I wondered if he was related to the lone farter in earlier the situation above? What is wrong with people?

A guy was eating a pan of BBQ ribs while driving, licking the sauce off his fingers and put them back on my steering wheel. Apparently, the thought of pulling over and eating them in a parking lot never occurred to him. How was in traffic was a much safer option? Initially, I thought he might be running late, hence the reason to eat one of the sloppiest meals in existence on the road. When he took a four-hour nap in a parking lot, I realized this guy was just a fucking idiot. He also licked off more BBQ sauce from his fingers after waking up from his slumber.

9.

One Year

S he showed up early in the morning, just a little after sunrise. It had been a slow month at the airport. I had only been out for a couple of days in the previous few weeks. Those were boring rentals with boring people too. While it was nice to get a break every so often to relax, look at planes taking off and landing in the distance, airport employees standing around doing nothing, that only served to amused me for so long. As much as I complain about some people and their existence, it was always good to get out more often. Even if I continued to drive around the same city, seeing the same things I did most of the time.

She stood out, mostly because she was a bit of a little thing. Probably not much taller than five feet in height. Wearing cargo shorts and boots. She did have a glow to her, a big smile while looking down at her rental agreement and eyeballing the spot where I was at. She had one of those huge backpacks

I have seen people carry when they go on long trips. Everything packed into one bag. I liked her attitude off the bat with that smile.

She looked right at me and said, "Hey! I found you!" It was stating the obvious, yes, you did, but as I have said before, I always liked people with a good happy attitude. She seemed to fit that profile quickly.

"You ready to go on an adventure?" she asked me directly. Unable to answer, I wanted to say yes, I am. I'm ready to get out. The last few trips I only went out on was to a convention center close to the airport and sat inside another boring parking garage. Smelled worse than the one at the airport. Before that, it was a stimulating ride out to the suburbs where I sat, and in three days all I had to amuse me was watching a neighbor cut their lawn, a dog piss on the side of a fence, and two high school kids get into a fight. Yeah, at this point, I'm ready for anything. Well, anything other than a grocery store or boring office building would be a refreshing change of pace for me.

She put her backpack in my passenger seat before getting in to start me up. It was heavy. Before leaving, she made a phone call and grinned when the other line picked up. "Mom, dad!" She said, "Yes, I just made it in. Yup, safe and sound." I could not make out what her parents were saying, but at least she let them know where she was. It was the typical banter where people let their families know they arrived at their destination safely. For some reason, I always found it amusing when people called other people to tell them they did not perish on whatever voyage it was they were on. If they did, I was sure they would be notified by the proper authorities in given time.

I could tell by the literature she had with her where we were going. The Grand Canyon. Big hole in the ground. Sweet! Another place I had heard so much about and had not had a chance to see yet.

After a little over an hour of driving up north, she pulled off the side of the highway. One of the scenic viewing areas that were common in Arizona. A place for motorists to stop for a few minutes to stretch, get a drink, maybe take a leak, and soak in a view. When she pulled off, she did not get out. Only turned off the ignition and sat silent for a few minutes looking at the scenery. She closed her eyes and started breathing deeply and slowly. This went on for a few minutes. While I was slightly concerned that this was a medical situation, she put my mind at ease when she started talking out loud. Almost like there was an invisible passenger with us.

"One year," she said, "It has been one year today since I made the decision. One year of my life back. One year ago, when I decided I had enough. Enough of it. One year ago today was when I became sober."

Shit. This was deep. I did not see it coming.

After saying that, she sat for a few more minutes, just looking out in front of her. The view. The view was gorgeous. A huge mountain was in front of us, and a valley below. A slight breeze had the bushes outside the highway pull-out swaying, bringing on the smell of the desert. A few flowers were even growing from the bushes. She just sat there and enjoyed it.

After a while, she opened up a pocket in her backpack and pulled out a small notebook. One no more than six inches in length and diameter with some stickers on the front. Clearly, well used as the cover had seen some better days. Scratches and dents on it. Stickers of horses, hummingbirds, and cats playing with balls of yarn covered the front and back. She opened it up and started to read from it silently. Initially, I was unaware of what was inside this book. But she smiled as she continued to read it. At one time, she even giggled at an entry within.

With that, she closed the notebook, placed it in the passenger seat next to her backpack, and fired up my ignition. "Let's start making out way to the canyon!" she said enthusiastically. And then we were back on the road. The Grand Canyon, from what I have gathered, was about a four-hour drive from Phoenix. I had only seen an advertisement banner for it in the airport, I was happy that this was going to be something new for me as well. From what I had learned, it was a "wonder of the world," whatever that means. But it was supposed to be a breathtaking view. Something that could not be put into words. It had to be seen to understand its beauty. If it drew as many people out there as I had heard, then I was looking forward to seeing it. I love new things. Plus, she continued to be upbeat. Also, to go through one year of a new life, being sober was an amazing achievement, from what I understood. Good on her.

A few hours later, we arrived at a smaller town about an hour or so south of the Grand Canyon. A town called Williams, Arizona. As I had learned earlier about the historic Route 66, this town made no effort to hide the fact they were on that same road.

I could also say this was not my first time on this road, but it was great to see another part of it. Neon signs were everywhere advertising their wares to sell. A complete road filled with neon. She pulled into a motel, went into the office and came out with her key. It was one of the standard motel rooms where the price seemed the be the goal before luxury. Everybody stayed in those. You know what was on this motel? Neon.

She took her backpack into the room, but she neglected to bring her notebook with her. It was still on my passenger seat. While grabbing her backpack, she knocked the notebook onto the floor, displaying some open pages she had written inside. I was pretty sure she had forgotten about it. While this was something deeply personal, and I knew I should not pry, it was right there for me to see. I decided maybe a quick peek, just to get a glimpse of what made her giggle a bit earlier. Just a quick view. Having no discipline myself, I read the page that was open. The first page inside her notebook.

"Today is the first day. Today is the day I start a new and better life. Today is the day I live without alcohol. From every day forward, I will go without it. If I cannot do this, then I cannot do life. In the first year, I will do all of the following:" And it listed several items. Do I keep reading? Do I leave this very personal entry for her only? Of course, I read it. Partially because I had no manners and partially because I wanted to see what she had written down that would make her life worthwhile. And largely, even though we were newly acquainted, I was proud of her.

- Take an hour each day to be by myself and remember why I am doing this new life

- Go see my favorite football team in Texas. Go to the game. Bring Sally from High School

- Make amends. This listed three people whom I had no idea who they were

- Walk across the Golden Gate Bridge in San Francisco, California

- Drive to the southernmost point in Key West, Florida. Send the picture to my sister

- See Mom and Dad at least once a week, call them every day

- Spend a night in Mackinac Island, Michigan

- Get a dog

- Go back to school

- Keep a job for more than 6 months

- Do my laundry every week

- Go to the Rock and Roll Hall of Fame in Ohio

- Cook dinner for myself every night I am not out of town. Clean the dishes right away.

- Learn to paddleboard

And the last entry, the only one not crossed off: "See and hike the Grand Canyon in Arizona. Watch a sunrise and sunset there. Do this one year after staying sober."

This trip was the last on the list. The Grand Canyon. Everything else had been crossed off. She did them all. It was so incredible to be on the final part of her journey.

She was up very early the next morning, two hours before the sun was up. A spring in her step, she was so energetic that early in the day. The same way she was when she came to pick me up the day before yesterday, with the same glow to her. Same smile. She wasted no time walking over to me and jumping in my driver's seat. "Good morning, car!" she said, with great energy. "Well, today is the day. The last thing on my list." I could see why she was so excited. The completion of this journey she had been on ended that day. And I was glad I read what the list was. Otherwise, I would have no idea what the hell she was talking about.

We made our way up to the southern part of the Grand Canyon an hour or so before the sun rose. She parked in a lot that was about as close to the canyon as we could be. I supposed waking up that early in the morning had its perks. We beat traffic and got a good parking spot. From there, she got out and leaned up against my passenger side door, looking east. She took her notebook out and opened it up to that first page I was able to see the night before. She probably read that list fifty times over again. I never really learned which item made her laugh before. I could only assume there was a story to one of those that I will never learn. Something that happened on her journey to get to where she was at. And that was all right.

As the sun started to rise, she spoke, "You know, I did it. I made it." She looked back down at her notebook and scrolled through a few pages again. It was too quick for me to really see what she had written in it past the first page. She stopped in the middle of the notebook, and all that was in there was one picture. It was her. One that was taped to a page. Above it was a date written down, one year ago from the day before. Sure, I could tell it was her, but a shell of this person I was with now. She looked sad. She looked depressed. There were bags around her eyes. Half asleep. Dirty clothes. Matted hair. She looked like shit. It was a lifestyle then. It was evident.

Her finger traced the chin of her own picture, looking at it. "I can't believe this was me. I can't believe who I had become." Then she was silent but smiling. She should smile. This was what I could only imagine was one hell of a task to get through. She took her life back. Having a life that was hers again. "There's no way I can take back what I have done and what I had lost, but I started over again. You know what car; I wake up every day happy." She was talking to me directly, as so many people do. I was happy to be there to listen. "I was never happy before. Alcohol gave me something to do, but it never really made me content. It just got me through a day. Then it ruined my life. Ten years. I just turned thirty-five last month. That was the first time I remember my family singing happy birthday to me in ten years. When I showed up, I was there, but never really there. I forgot how my mom's voice sounded singing that and how happy my dad was bringing in my cake to me with a candle for every year I've been alive. The way he was always proud of me no matter what I did. Watched me open up the presents they bought me. What great parents they are. The terrible job my dad always did at wrapping presents, but he was so happy watching me open them up. How happy they were to do that. It is sad to think of the Christmas nights I missed because I was too hungover to go to their house. How I missed my nephew being born because I was out at the bar. How many jobs I lost because I could not show up on time."

It was that moment where I saw people take inventory on their life. Then she shifted to the positives she had the year before. The smile came back

72

more with each moment that passed. "You know, I show up to work every day fifteen minutes early now? Every day. I'm never late anymore. Never a missed family event or party. Not a single one. They are so much fun to be around! You know, I bought a goddamn meat smoker out of the blue and just learned how to smoke meat. Just decided to do it one day. I hosted my dad's retirement party with that a few months back. Huge party! Everyone was there! I have done so much in this last year."

She fell silent, looked down at her feet, and then back up at the rising sun, "It was all these little things that I missed before. They're not so little. Every day means something to me now. I have not wasted three-hundred and sixty-five days in a row, car. Not a single one of them. Now three-hundred and sixty-six. I made it over a year." She smiled, looked at me and back at the view. "It was the parties with my family are the ones that mattered. Not being out with people I don't know, blacking out, and forgetting about what I did the night before, only to wake up and start drinking again to get over the hangover. The parties with my family and real friends, going out to see things, being together. I helped my dad put up Christmas lights last season and forgot how much fun that was. How we could normally get it done in an hour or two, but we would spend all day listening to Christmas music and hearing my dad sing completely off-key the entire time. Going out with my nephew on Halloween trick-or-treating, watching him do his best to try and stop tripping on his costume. Yeah, those are the best times, the best parties, car."

We sat there together, and she fell silent again for a bit, taking in the view and morning air. Once the sun had fully risen, she pulled more papers from her bag, revealing her plans. She was going to take a bus to the north rim of the Grand Canyon and spend the night there. Then make the twenty-plus plus mile hike back to the south rim back to me. That was a ton of miles. Some people that have rented me have not even driven that much in a day. This was hiking down and back up the canyon. It also meant that I was going to be sitting there all day today and most of tomorrow. There could be worse places to stay put for a while. I would get all that time to take in the views. I was fine with that.

With that, she was off to catch her bus. I watched as more people came into the parking lot throughout the morning. Families go off to spend some time there; tour company busses drop off hordes of people on vacation. I had never seen so many brown bag lunches, cameras, fanny packs, and water bottles in my life. But everyone seemed happy to be there. To see something this amazing. I liked the joy that came out of it from people.

A few hours later, I heard a train come in. One that left the same place we stayed at the night before, in the town of Williams. It was bringing hundreds of people on a vintage ride up to the canyon. The sound of the train coming up the tracks and the whistle blowing. The chugging sound the engine made going on the tracks. It reminded me of the same sounds I heard right after I was brand new, making my way to Arizona. My train ride out. I wonder what that would have been like many, many decades before when car travel was not as common, a train may have been one of the only ways for people to come up and see the views here. I learned from so many people walking by that the train had been there forever. I had never really seen trains up that close, just passing by them on highways and interstates previously. I was glad I was there.

Night came as quickly as the sun did. A largely empty parking lot by now. The only cars there were from people staying the night or doing the same thing my driver did and took a bus across the canyon to make that hike. Everybody else was gone. The train that came up made its way back hours ago south to Williams. It made me think about my driver and how excited she was about this. How tomorrow would be such an amazing day for her. Not only to hike the canyon all the way across but to make that change in her life. As soon as she finished that hike, she would have completed her year-long list. Where would she be now if she did not make that decision? What kind of path would she be on now? Would she still be alive?

The sun rose the next morning as it always does. At this time, I knew she had already started her hike. Her details had her beginning the trek a few hours before the sun came up. I guess this was necessary to make the entire hike in one day.

It came to that part of the day, when the sun dipped over the horizon within about thirty minutes when I saw her again. At dusk. With all I had seen in her absence, I had almost forgotten to keep an eye out for her to come back, but I still thought of her often. In between another busy day in the parking lot. I wondered what she was seeing inside the canyon. What did the views look like from the bottom of it? Was she alone or meeting new friends walking with her? How was she doing with that huge backpack she brought? Did she put on enough sunscreen before leaving? Was she drinking enough water? Had she seen the river that runs down there? Was this the hike she envisioned? Were there any bears or other wild animals she has to worry about?

At this time, I almost understood the irony when she called her parents to let them know she arrived in Arizona safe, how much I made fun of her for that. I wished I had a quick call to let me know she was doing well on the trail and was almost done and would be back to me soon. But I did not have a phone. Now I got why people did this. I cared about her. I felt like a parent to her. She deserved that.

She had a new glow to her when she came into view. That look of accomplishment that was only seen from something like this adventure, not surviving another day at work. She set her backpack down next to me and let out the loudest "Woo-Hoo!" I had ever heard in my existence. "I did it!" she yelled out.

Seeing her so happy was like getting a fresh oil change. Two guys twenty years her senior who were getting into a car a few lanes down, realizing what she did, approached her, offering a proper high five and praise for such an accomplishment. It was obvious by her appearance that she made the entire hike from rim to rim. Dirty and tired. She leaned against my driver's side door, the opposite side from what she had done the previous day when she watched the sunrise to now watch the sunset. I did not even care if she was wearing or scratching my paint a bit by doing that.

She pulled out a soda bottle from her bag, cracked the top off, and took a huge sip. All gone in two huge gulps. Before the light completely faded, she looked over at the canyon, still never taking her eyes off it completely. I could only assume thinking about her ambitious feat while seeing the Grand Canyon. A year ago, would not have been able to or even think about doing it. She sat there silently, never losing her smile, just watched the sun drift lower and lower. The notebook was pulled out again, and she opened it back up to the first page and took a pen out from her bag. In one big move, she crossed off "See and hike the Grand Canyon in Arizona" from the list. Right there next to me.

As soon as the sun was out of sight, only giving light from under the horizon, she quietly said, "I did it. I am OK. I am going to be OK."

We made our drive back to the same hotel she had stayed at two nights before in Williams. She barely had enough energy left in her to make the drive, but she did it. Poor girl could barely keep her eyes open. The feeling from her accomplishment kept her going.

Two days before, she still had one item on the list. It was funny to think about how one item on a sheet of paper could make so much of a difference. I understood it was more than that and how much had to go into planning this, but being able to cross that off the list on this trip was monumental.

The next morning, I did not see her at sunrise, and with just cause. She needed the rest and came out in the late morning with her same backpack. She had more color in her face from all the sun she got the day before. On the drive back to Phoenix, she pulled off to the side of the road at the same overlook she made on the way up, about an hour north of Phoenix. At that same gorgeous view we saw a few days before. It was almost going back in time.

She shut the ignition off and sat there, taking in the scenery again. The same bushes from before were swaying in the light breeze on the side of the road. The same little flowers that grew near the bushes were still there. The same valley. She took her notebook out of the backpack and put it on her lap. She did not open it right away, just put her hand on it for a few minutes. Tapping it with her index finger a few times. She slowly turned her head to look out amongst the view at a small rain cloud in the distance. I was sure I heard a slight rumble of thunder coming from it. There were a few times she opened the cover up to the notebook, only to close it. After a sigh, she moved towards the back of it, past the picture of herself she had taken a year before and grabbed her pen. She took the first empty page and at the top wrote: CHAPTER TWO. YEAR TWO.

While I would normally divulge everything as there was no legal recourse to sue a car over slander, that one stays between us. What she wrote in there was a laundry list of what she would do in the next year with her life. There were no repeats from year one. This was a whole new list of adventures she was going to do and ways to continue to make her life spectacular. About the same size list as the first page of her book. The first year. With new places to visit, more people to connect with, and new things to learn. No, that was for her. I would only say I hoped she completed the next year of things she wanted to do as well. All of it. It was ambitious again, the same as her first year, but after seeing what she had done already before in the last year, the first year of sobriety, I had no doubt it would be accomplished. No doubt at all.

The only thing she wrote on there I would share was the last thing on her list for year two. Create Chapter three. Year three. It was the last thing on the list.

You go, girl.

We eventually ended up back at the airport to drop me off. Another adventure in the books. For both of us. As she took her backpack out of the front seat, she did what most people do when dropping me off. Scour everything inside to make sure they did not forget anything. It shocks me how many possessions were left in me. She really did not have much other than that huge backpack and what was in it. But she did something that made me feel more connected to her. She never opened up my trunk the entire trip until she dropped me off. Not once. Going through it just to check, she took her hair clip off, revealing long dark brown hair which had been tied up the entire trip. I never saw how long it was until now. She tussled it a bit to give it more volume, as she let it down. She said in a quiet voice to me, "Hey, you never know who is going to be on the plane ride home, right? A girl has to look good! Thank you for getting me there. This is for you!"

With a smile, she attached the hair clip in a spot towards the back of my trunk. Virtually impossible to find if you did not know it was there. On the back of some of the upper part of my trunk liner carpet. There were still elements of deer blood back there from the previous "incident" that took place. "In case you need it!" she added with a smile as she closed my trunk.

I usually got pretty irritated most of the time when people left anything inside me, especially on purpose. This one was different. She was leaving a little part of her with me. It was not until she walked away that I realized that it was the same hair clip she had in the picture she took of herself just over a year ago. The one that had a butterfly on top. How transformed one year made this girl look. Yeah, I was happy to hold that for her. The quick time we had together would be a part of me forever. Or at least until someone found it. I hoped nobody ever does. Hoped she would get to write year fifty. And then some.

10.

The Family Vacation

"Yeah, this is not what we put our reservation in for. This is completely wrong."

This was starting out beautiful. Sarcasm. I continued to learn this word well.

The rental car agent looked at the paperwork without a single care in the world. Then looked at me. "Yeah, you guys were supposed to get a minivan. I do apologize, we were overbooked, and this is the largest vehicle we have available. It is a holiday weekend, you know."

I watched the back-and-forth between the two of them for several minutes. Eventually he accepted the keys and started to head home. I kept seeing him look at my back seats, looking in the rearview mirror, and constantly telling himself, "This car is way too small" over and over.

This was going to be a fun trip. The sarcasm again.

He drove us home to a woman setting out all their things for the trip from the garage. All camping equipment. I assumed this was the mom. I could also see why I was not the ideal choice; there were way more things than would fit inside me. I did not take this personally. Then as an added bonus, it was not just him and his wife. I saw two kids smiling, then changing their facial expressions to what seemed to be a healthy blend of sorrow and confusion at my presence.

His wife approached him "Um...honey, we were supposed to get a minivan. What in the hell is this? We can't fit in here with the kids and all the stuff."

Then the deep sigh I heard all people make in these scenarios, "Yeah, Hun, they were overbooked. This is all that was available. I had them check the other companies. All vans are already out. This is our only option. Let's just pack up the car and get going, I already had to dick around for close to an hour before leaving with this pile."

I saw the mom look up at him, doing her best to contain a bit of a smile at the situation. He was not as successful, gave a bit of a chuckle, and said "Hey, it will work out. I'm sure it'll be a complete disaster, but that will make for a good story at our kid's weddings. Come on, let's go. Traffic is already getting heavy."

His wife looked back at the bags set out and said comedically, "Sure, what half of all of these things should we leave behind?" They seemed to be taking to assess their situation with a bit of humor. I loved humor, especially when most people resorted to anger, which typically resulted in them taking it out on me.

The next hour or so consisted of them making calculated decisions on what to leave behind. It was a mix of certain essentials, like they "could" make one jacket for each person last all week, two of the three coolers were discarded from the inventory, the brand-new portable table with a $199 price tag was moved back into the garage and the fishing equipment with an equal dollar amount went back to storage. In an amazing feat of geometry, some camping equipment, clothing, a decent amount of food, and a few recreational items were able to fit. The husband and wife sat in the front, and two kids were in the back seat. It was a perfectly constructed display of space management.

About a mile away, they pulled off to fill up the gas tank as the last renter failed to do so and was charged appropriately. The dad got out, paid at the pump, and looked into me at his family. A small genuine smile popped out from him, watching his son and daughter in the back seat laughing and carrying on as kids do. Coloring books and all sorts of other crap piled on them. They were still young enough where they liked being around each other, before the early teenage years, that I came to understand was complete hell otherwise known as adolescence, where they are just pissed off all the time and hated everything and listened to music that reflected it.

The mom got out and walked over to him. "Hey, are you all right?" she asked.

He took a few seconds and then looked at her with direct eye contact, "You know, this car is too small. We really don't have the money for this right now, anyhow. Why don't we just go up to my parent's place a few hours away? Stay there for a few days and come back home. Get back to reality sooner. I just think this isn't a good time to take this trip, with me getting laid off. Let's just take another year. Let me get a new job, get a little more stable, and we can do this trip the way it should be."

She held his gaze and said, "Look, I love you. We planned this six months ago and it is all the kids have been talking about for the last few weeks. Our summer trip. We are all right; my job is still doing well, we have some savings, and the bills are still getting paid. All of the camping gear was bought months ago. We'll be all right. You need this time off. We've missed you so much because of work, and that job is done. Your kids miss you. I miss you. And when are we going to get this much time off again, just the four of us? You don't have to check into work, you don't have to leave for thirty minutes to help a client. Just take this time, be back with your family. That is all you need to do right now"

"Seriously, what would I do without you?"

She smiled back at him, boosting a huge smile, and said, "You would worry too much! Look at those kids in the back seat."

He glanced over, the two of them still laughing and looking at a map of their trip. Calling out all the cities and towns they would pass on their journey. Giggling about a sixteen-hour drive. Constantly smiling as kids that age did.

She stood next to him and put her hands around him, and they took a few seconds, just looking at them. "Next year, our son in the third grade and daughter will be in sixth grade. Her first year of Middle School. We'll never get this time back. It will all work out."

The gas pump then clicked to indicate my tank was full. He smiled back at her, replaced the pump, and sealed my gas cap back on. "That's our sign, babe. Let's go!"

The first day was a long drive, all the way from Phoenix to northern Utah. It was rewarding. The kids never stopped having fun in the back seat. Never complained. The two young ones made it a point to give as many names as possible to the animals they saw. When they would see cows in a pasture, they would roll the window down and make a "Mooing" sound at them. No matter how many times they did it, they kept laughing. I am not sure if Gary was a common name for a dairy cow, but one on the side of the road was assigned that designation. It was reassuring, though, and healthy seeing a family enjoy that time together.

After the sun went down, they kept driving, only pulling out a sheet of paper for a motel they had set up that night. The dad looked tired. The mom looked tired. The kids in the back seat had long since fallen asleep a few hours before their arrival. That was it for the day. A long drive and some well-deserved sleep for them.

They were up early the next day, very early. The sun came up so primal in the summer, and they were up with it. They packed the few things they took into the motel room the night before back into my exceptionally crammed trunk. I was still amazed they fit in as much as they did. I heard them talking about getting an early start to get to Yellowstone with enough time to enjoy their first day. The kids returned to the back seat, feasting on a makeshift breakfast of nothing but the finest of the continental breakfast at a budget motel. Expired fruit, stale toast, and milk slightly cooler than room temperature. The mom and dad seemed to only be interested in consuming coffee at that time. I got that.

Only a few hours later and already well into Idaho, the scenery changed dramatically. I could make out huge mountains in the distance, and probably the most gorgeous landscape I had seen up until that point was there for us all to take in. Those mountains, how green the trees were.

We pulled into a sliver of Montana, and we were there. Yellowstone National Park. For something that had been there for so long, I would assume that it was known how busy this park got and the amount of people who wanted to enjoy this area in the summer. Since I had to find something to complain about all the time, the line to get in was excessive. Ninety minutes later, we were in. However, if we were stuck in a line anywhere, that place was the one to do it in. Somewhere so gorgeous. Even watching a deer stop to take a dump by the side of the road. Elegant. The kids laughed at it. Then named the deer "Scott". We get the map of the park and some exceptionally unclear directions on the quickest way to get to the campsite from the park ranger.

They drove up to their assigned spot at the campsite. It was not a bad space; a nice flat location cleared out and a spot for the tent. A picnic table and a small fire ring to call home for the next few nights. Big, tall trees everywhere.

We pulled into the space, the kids in the back of the car started to get more energy. I heard the daughter ask, "Mom, Dad, is this our spot?" with the curious and ambitious energy that comes with kids.

"Yup, this is it, baby!" the dad informed her. The kids were the first out of the car, running out to explore their surroundings. Both of them laughed and stared up at trees that, in the imagination of kids that reached all the way to heaven. The parents slowly got out of the car and looked over at the two kids exploring their area. The mom leaned up against the dad; they watched over at their kids for a while and pulled the energy from their excitement.

"This is going to be a really great experience." the mom said decisively.

Sometimes too much of a good thing can present a problem, as one speedbump that should come along brings you back to reality. Or several speedbumps. This became clear once the unpacking process and setting up of the camp they would call home for the next five nights began.

We were having such a good time beforehand. While the kids were off running around the base of the trees, burning off the energy they had remaining, mom and dad were left to the task of assembling what would be their accommodations for the next several nights. My trunk popped open, and the parents looked inside.

"I can't believe we were able to cram all this shit inside of here. I need a crowbar to get anything out," the dad joked. I would give them that, they did unload my trunk and systematically lay everything out in a line to see what they had to work with. They even paid careful attention to ensure they did not scratch up my paint. Much appreciated. "That camping stove with the griddle I ordered. That would have been really nice to have. So glad we just bought it for it to sit in the garage, no doubt to be forgotten about for the next several years and sold at a garage sale for six bucks. What did we spend on that again?" he asked.

"Two hundred and fifty. Two hundred and fifty dollars," the mom said with a teasing smile.

"Ahhhh, yes, that is right. Money well spent," the dad muttered, giving the same smile back at his wife.

I would hand it to them, for as many things that they left behind and their situation, they were taking it with humor. I have seen couples get into fights over what restaurant to go to with the hostility that would make a pack of wolverines concerned. These two seemed to take a much more difficult situation in stride, just going with the situation and making good family memories.

Seeing as how they left on their trip abandoning half of the camping supplies they planned for, I would say they did a pretty good job having the essentials. Except for one critical component that no doubt would set the tone for their first night's sleep. Perhaps every night on this journey. The tent poles. Scrambling around looking for them, I saw the back-and-forth questions of, "Are you sure we put those in the trunk?" It was asked no less than a dozen times. A time of fear when I saw people try to think of something so much that they believed it would come true.

Yet, no amount of faith can miracle an object to appear out of nowhere. After looking in my empty trunk over and over, pulling up the spare tire compartment in a last hope of desperation that something so large would have rolled into a crevice only to be discovered with a sigh of relief. This was not their reality. After bringing the kids over to ask if they had moved them or hid them somewhere in the car, the realization set in that they were left at home. Probably sitting on the side of the house in a spot that would ensure they were not forgotten but inevitably were. Yup. They forgot the tent poles. Hey, but at least they had the tent. Basically, having a car with no engine. You were not going to get far.

I noticed that people do become resilient at certain times, and creativity does lead to some great feats. If people were not curious and ambitious, I myself as a car, would have never been conceived and constructed. The ambition to create was amazing with people. Just look at airplanes.

The family scanned the nearby forest and found downed tree limbs that were an approximate size of the absent tent poles. With about an hour of time, half a roll of duct tape, and some thin cord borrowed by a neighboring campsite, a haphazard shelter loosely resembling a tent was constructed. It looked as if a two-mile-an-hour wind would blow it over, or even the simple act of stepping in the tent would upset the delicate balance of this would-be-shelter.

"See, it's fine. It'll work," the dad said.

The mom tapped the top of it, and the smallest amount of force saw the cord holding up the back of the tent tied to a tree slip down a good twelve inches. They took a step back to survey their house of cards quickly falling. Without any intervention, their efforts were in vain as gravity saw their work crumble to the ground. It just fell on its own. They just stood there, not saying a word. Stared at it. Both were doing their best to contain their laughter as they had done already on this trip multiple times. This time, it was unsuccessful. They both broke out in hysterics. I would say it again; they had the right attitude for this adventure before them.

The kids came back and listened to the most awkward explanation of how they were going to sleep on top of the tent in their sleeping bags so they could fall asleep looking up at the stars. Kids that age seemed to go with just about anything and did not seem to care. They were even a bit excited at that.

They got a fire going, made some sandwiches, and settled on a blanket next to each other without any chairs, as they were back home, safely tucked in the garage. All things considered; they did not seem to mind. They were just together as a family doing what they should while camping and listening to their kids tell wild tales of their imagination, talking about their plans for the rest of the trip and all the things they would see. Mom and dad made up ghost stories on the fly, only to be interrupted by the kid's occasional screams. They ate a lot of S'mores, whatever the hell those were.

As the evening went on, they put their kids into their sleeping bags, concerned about being out in the elements but reassuring themselves that no one would die and they would survive the night just fine. With the kids safely tucked into their sleeping bags and falling asleep, the mom motioned for dad to come to the side of the car. She revealed the "contraband" in a packed bag she smuggled. A single pint of whiskey, his favorite brand. "Well, come over with me back to the fire. Let's have a drink together."

He smiled back at her and said, "You know sure as hell, we will need to drink that entire bottle just to be able to fall asleep tonight."

"Why do you think I brought it? I knew there would be some reason we'd need it." she replied, still never losing that smile.

They spent the next two hours or so together, sitting at my side, talking quietly as they took sips off the plastic liquor bottle. All the while, they kept their voices down as they they reminisced about their lives together, the first house they bought with everything they had, stealing light bulbs from one room to put into another and waiting for the next payday to replace them, how excited they were when they first found out they were going to be parents, and all other great times they had over the years. How they still find time to take a quick dance in the kitchen together when making dinner.

They looked over every few minutes to check on their kids, who were still sound asleep, and then they carried on. These two were still in love, and it showed. With the bottle dry, as quiet as two people who were noticeably drunk can be, they made their way back to the kids and slid into their sleeping bags with the two kids in between them. That slight drunk giggle came from each of them, but they were still tactful enough not to wake up the children.

Yeah, these two were going to make it for life. Good on them.

The next morning seemed to have reality kick in. Early. Much earlier than planned. With the slight crack of the sun rising, I hear the mom give a moan of discomfort, waking Dad up to mimic in the same fashion of grunting instead of talking. It sounded like two mammals communicating under water. They were slow to sit up, eyes puffy as they took in the reality around them.

"I think I'm still drunk." she said to him.

"I know, undeniably, I'm definitely still drunk. Shit." he spoke. They looked over to see their kids still sound asleep, barely able to see their eyes above the tops of the sleeping bags. "This tent situation needs to be addressed, one more night sleeping like that, and I'm turning in my resignation on this trip." The dad said. I wasn't sure if he was kidding or not.

"Agreed." mom replied, with no energy in her voice. They eventually pulled a skillet out of the meager belongings with them and opened the one cooler to get started on some breakfast. The coals from the fire the night before were adequate to heat up the pan and they put in everything they had. Eggs, bacon, sausage, hash browns. No separation.

I can still smell a bit of the whiskey on their breath. But I harbor no judgement on that.

A fellow camper came walking by. An older gentleman with a cup of coffee with a "World's Greatest Old Fart" on the front of it was walking a tiny dog and invited himself into their campground and made the obvious comment "Looks like there is something wrong with your tent."

"Yeah," the mom said, "We forgot our tent poles at home. Did the best we could for last night. We will figure something out today. Thanks." She added politely while doing her best not to lead on with the annoyance of only being awake for five minutes and someone stating what is evident.

"Well, you can't put up a tent without tent poles," he said.

"Yeah, we kind of figured that out last night; thanks, we'll get it taken care of," the mom told him, her voice getting tenser with each word.

Without an invitation, he sat down on a tree stump in their campsite. The small dog was barking and baring its teeth at the mom and dad the entire time. He was ignoring it, probably the same way he did his last cholesterol test. The old man started talking like the barking dog did not exist, going into the biology of a tent, making the analogy of how tent poles are the skeleton of the structure, and without that, it was just loose skin.

The mom was taking deep breaths, doing her best to be polite. But she was pissed. The old man was oblivious to her annoyance. I was also quite miffed. The dog was still barking, now waking up the kids. It staggered the imagination to think of what makes this little animal so full of anger and hate. Probably from being around the old man too much. I could fathom that.

He was completely unaware that nobody really wanted him around. The kids woke up and walked to the campfire, all the while the old man continued talking. The mom started to dish out their breakfast for them while the old man was still talking over them constantly, telling them about his road trip. Even when the kids asked where their drinks were, that did not slow the old man down. He started going on about a tire repair he had the week before. He thought he paid too much for it because it was usually twenty dollars less in the city. Nobody cared.

He was talking over the entire family; there was no comprehension that they had been awake for less than a few minutes while hungover as all hell and had two hungry kids to take care of. With the family getting close to being done eating, the old man finally left, telling them he would only be there for one more night. Like they gave a shit.

"I was going to punt that dog into the fucking fire if he stayed here one more minute. Then hold that man's head next to it and make him watch that barking malignant spirit burn," the dad whispered to his wife.

"Oh my God, my head is pounding so hard. Every time my heart beats, I can feel the pulse of it inside my brain. Every bark from that fresh hell of a dog felt like I was being punished for something I'm not aware of."

After getting the camp straightened out, everybody fed and things put away, the question remained from what I had now called "The Tent Situation." It was in the low thirties last night, cold. Sure, one night, no problem, but they were not going to get through the week doing that again. The liquor was not that strong, and it was finished.

They took a look at their park map and saw a general store a few miles down the road. The dad decided to run out quickly to see about fixing their living arrangements for the next few nights. Knowing it was going to be quicker alone, he ran out solo to the shop. It was inside a National Park, not exactly the biggest general store known to man, but stocked with supplies most would need out camping that were already back in their garage at home. Beer, liquor, hot dogs, bread, milk, soda, and an assortment of camping supplies. Scouring inside, he found the missing item needed. Universal tent poles.

He climber back into my driver's seat and put the purchase on my passenger seat. I saw the cost of forgetting what they already had back outside at their house if it has not already been stolen by someone in the neighborhood, "Universal Tent Poles." The price was tag: $100. He looks at his purchase on my passenger seat and mutters one word. "Fuck." If I did not like this family, I would find this pretty funny. When he got back to the campsite, the mom and kids worked together, and the tent poles they bought seemed to be adjustable, making for a quicker task in getting their tent set up. So quickly, in fact, I saw mom and dad looking at it like it was too good to be true. Questioning their situation, they even lightly push up against the tent. The shape remained. Sturdy. As many things as they had going against them, this one was a victory. Mom and dad high-fived each other in the victory. I was happy because I thought they were still a little too hungover to do much more than that.

On the first day, we took a short drive around the park. Not too far away was a pretty big lake they figured would be a great place to do some swimming and enjoy the weather. It turned into a really comfortable late morning as far as the weather was concerned. A few clouds were in the sky and a slight breeze. They made their way partially around the lake and found a spot designated for people to pull off and use the water. The kids were excited, even if all of their floating toys were left back at their house. They did not seem to care when they saw what was in front of them. Before getting into the water, they even saw a bald eagle that the son pointed out to all of them. Just sitting on the branch of a tree. Son and daughter, true to the fashion on the trip, named the bald eagle "Jeff." I loved the imagination of kids.

The next few hours consisted of them and many other campers taking advantage of the day and the water. Families were swimming, and people were lying out on the side of the water reading, taking a nap, making lunch, and drinking cheap overpriced canned beer hidden in brown paper bags. A few men out in the distance on the other side of the water were attempting to catch fish away from the commotion and noise of said beachgoers. Everybody looked like they were having a great time. Kids who had never met each other were playing games in the water like they had been friends for years. The adults occasionally cooled off by getting into the water to spend time with their offspring. I was able to watch most of this as everything was still in sight of me. It was nice seeing all those people enjoy themselves, having a good time on a summer vacation.

We returned to the camp later that afternoon. Everybody was exhausted from their day out but was reminiscing on the fun times they had. The dad got another fire started for the night as the rest of the family sat around eating sandwiches and talking about their next day. They really did not have too many plans and left it open to the kids to set up the next day. Both of them said they wanted to walk around and see the trails and animals around their campsite.

The sun went down shortly after, and I had to say that in this park, it got really cold fast after the sun went down. Really fast. They sat close to the fire and repeated a lot of what they had done the night before. They told more ghost stories and watched their dad walk around the campfire with a towel around his head while making up a story about a hunchback that lived in the same park in an endless quest to feast on children. He was doing his best to mimic what this creature may look like, and he listened to the kids give little screams the more dad acted like this creature. Screaming, but smiling. Again, it was another night they were having fun together.

Over the next few days I would like to say that they took me out and explored the entire park, looking at all there was to be offered. I would like to say that I was with them the entire time. Truth be told, for a few days, I just sat there at the campsite. Except for two quick trips back to the general store for more food, ice, and firewood I never moved. And it was all right. For local travel, they used the busses in the park to get around and see the sights. It was easier to see everything without having to worry about driving. They would wake up, eat, pack a lunch for later, walk around hiking on their own adventures, and come back in the early evenings to have dinner, and spend some time together, either quietly or telling stories before going to sleep.

It was just fine. Every day they came back over those few days, they were laughing and having a great time. I could always hear them about one hundred yards away making their way back. I got to know all four of their voices well by this point. I was just happy they were out having fun and making this trip into something unbelievable for themselves. It was nice hearing that at the end of the day. Talking about what they did and what they saw. It still made me feel like I was a part of their trip together.

On the third to the last day, I never drove them anywhere but did get to see this family all day. They seemed to get a bit of a later start, emerging from their tent to get breakfast starting after the sun rose. The dad looked up at the sky, and the clouds had a grey tint to them. Rolling slowly above us all; the temperature was much cooler than the other days. Very little sun was able to poke through.

"Shit. Rain." he said quietly.

The mom stared up at the same sky. "I don't think we are going to go out for a bit. Let's get the kids fed and anticipate this dumping on us." They woke the kids up to go to the bathroom, and the dad started looking for the raincoats and umbrellas they had.

After rummaging through my trunk, the dad said, "I think it is safe to assume that we left all the brand new, expensive rain gear at home, right?"

"Yup." the mom agreed.

"Well, another adventure for us. What the hell are we going to do?" the dad asked, hearing the first roll of thunder clouds in the distance. "Let's just finish breakfast quickly, get some cards, games, whatever we can find to keep the kids busy inside the tent."

The kids came back from the bathroom, and the family ate quickly. The sounds of thunder were becoming more frequent and increasing in volume. Loud claps of thunder. The temperature continued to slowly drop, and the winds increased. Thankfully, they planned ahead. After eating, they scurried to secure their belongings outside, preparing for the rain. The kids were ushered into the tent about one minute before the first drops of rain started to fall. And it escalated quickly. A quick initial drizzle was followed up by a complete downpour.

Inside the tent, I heard the kids laughing and saying, "Wow!" after each crash of thunder and I had to say it was the loudest I have ever heard thunder. There were no storms like this in Phoenix. The rain falling seemed to come down in buckets, and other campers in the area were not as quick to plan their strategy for this event. People ran around outside, desperately trying to get under cover; many hikers in the area ran to the nearby bathroom building, which only had about one foot of covered space for them to stand under, looking up at the sky that was futile against the wind blowing the rain on them. I saw the car across the way with the windows down, and the owners of it had left hours before to go on a hike. Inside of that car was getting soaked. I found humor in that for some odd reason. Probably because my windows were all the way up.

This went on for almost three hours. The intensity of the rain falling varied, from a light rain going back to a complete downpour where you could barely see in front of you. The family did not seem to mind. After the rain had quit falling, other nearby campers had learned that rain had soaked into their tents, thus wrecking any opportunity for a good night's sleep later on. The whole time, my family seemed to take it like everything else on this trip, in their stride. They watched the rain, watched other camper's belongings drift away in the little streams that the rain made, and all the other ill-prepared people in the losing battle trying to stay dry in an impossible situation. Nearby tents collapsed under the weight of the water falling on them. This family played games in the tent, told stories, and took in the beauty that the storm brought to the park and taking in the smell of the rain.

The second to last night was a bit of an adventure. In the middle of the night, things became entertaining. I saw a plethora of signs all over the park when we came in, repeating a lot of the same information: Store your food in a bear box or your car. The thought of a bear tearing me apart to get a box of toaster pastries and hamburger buns seemed a bit extreme, but I assumed they would not be welcome inside a store to purchase these items and would do what they deemed necessary to get a snack. I also doubted they had the required currency to purchase those items at any of the general stores anyway. Who would hire them? And they could care less about damaging any vehicles. They pay no insurance premiums. At least, that was my assumption. It was an overall losing situation. No, we did not see a bear. But we did have an unwelcome visitor.

I vividly remember it as if I heard a commotion, as I heard a commotion from inside the family's tent. "What in the hell was that?" I heard the mom say with a concerned tone. Followed by the sound of leaves being moved around and a few branches snapping under the weight of an animal. Even with the small fires still going from various camps, it was too dark to see what was coming out of the trees.

"What, what are you talking about?" asked the dad, with no concern in his voice, though a slight yawn.

"Something is out there. I heard something right next to the tent, walking around."

"It's probably one of those drunk guys a few sites down taking a piss. Don't worry about it." the dad replied back, still no empathy in his voice. I heard it again. The mom heard it again. More rustling around near the side of their tent.

"You need to get up and see what that is. That isn't someone taking a piss. There is nobody out there swearing like those guys have been doing all day. It's something else." the mom decided, her tone becoming more concerned.

"All right, I'll go take a look."

I heard the tent unzip and the sound of a flashlight click on, and he scanned the perimeter. Nothing. Then he heard it, the rustling of leaves from something shuffling their feet. Then a loud movement of something rummaging through camping gear near them. A thud as a hard object was knocked off a picnic table at the camp site next to them. I saw him perk up pretty quickly after that. Justifiably an inferior way to wake up. I was glad they were not hitting the liquor like they did the first night. They could have slept through this whole thing and been devoured, too passed out to do anything about it. He climbed fully out of the tent and zipped it shut behind him.

"Stay inside." He whispered to the mom. Knowing little about wildlife, I was unaware of the protocol when a wild animal entered your personal space.

"Oh shit!" I heard him say loudly, not observing the posted quiet hours.

"What, what is it?" the mom shouted, still never shaking the concern from her voice.

It was then I saw it. The flashlight fixed on to the glow of the eyes, the animal did not break the line of sight it had on the dad. This gave me enough light to see who the trespasser was. A skunk. I had only heard about these animals. I knew little of their species. When they were startled, threatened, harassed, mugged, or pissed off, they would emit a wet odor that sprayed in a fury, shooting out like some sort of diseased carwash on whatever threatened them. Sure, I had smelled this putrid stench before on highways, typically from a deceased skunk that was hit by a car. While having an effective stench fight mechanism, they were still not huge animals and were no match for a moving vehicle.

The dad stood there, motionless, still keeping the flashlight on the skunk. It was one of those moments where I saw people who knew the situation they are in, but unable to decide on the best course of action at the time.

Shock took over. The skunk stood still, staring back at him for a few more moments. Almost with a "Come at me, man!" look to it.

All the dad was able to muster at the time was to tell the mom, "It's a skunk. Stay inside the tent. I don't want this bastard to get scared and spray us."

Maybe that was just enough time for the skunk to realize that the dad was not a threat and go back to the primary goal of showing up to raid a campsite. The thud they heard previously was from the guests next to them and their cooler being knocked off the picnic table on the ground, removing the lid. Ice was spilled all over the ground, as well as the food inside. The cooler was busted all to hell. One of the cheap styrofoam ones that had a cartoon of a beaver on the side of it. The skunk took a quick inventory of the items presented on the ground and snagged a full package of hotdogs in its mouth. Excellent choice. It then departed back into the trees as quickly as it showed up. Completely out of sight. A real smash-and-grab theft.

After a good few minutes, all I hear was the dad say, "What the hell just happened?" with laughter in his voice. Starting to boost that chuckle, he had a little more, but quiet enough that it did not wake the kids up. I could hear the mom bury her face into his shoulder, answering back with the same chuckle, doing her best not to wake up the kids as well. This went on for a few minutes. This couple really seemed to take situations like this in their stride. I bet if the animal had sprayed them, we may have met their breaking point?

They woke up the next day on a few hours of sleep. I heard the grunts and sounds of mom and dad waking up. Followed by a lot more swearing than I had heard them do with the simple act of getting up. They got a pass after the events of the night before, but I had learned that they really were not morning people by nature.

Climbing out of the tent and surveyed the "crime scene" caused by the skunk, only to see all items of food gone from the neighboring campsite. All that remained were a few cubes of ice in the final stages of their melting point and a busted styrofoam cooler. It was all within clear site of one of the multiple signs informing campers to store their food in a bear box or their car.

Seeing as how I witnessed their next-door neighbors consume no less than about twenty cans of beer each evening per person, I could understand how they may have missed the signs. I supposed since nobody was sprayed by the skunk, the damage done by that animal was an acceptable loss. I had to say when the neighbors woke up with the dumfounded look on their faces, no food to soak up their hangover, little paw prints all over their campsite, and the confusion they had trying to put the pieces together of what happened through their ungodly loud snoring the night before looking at their cooler busted all to shit in the dirt… it made me laugh. At least, as much as a car could laugh.

The family planned their final full day with a hiking trail that they were looking forward to the most. It was a day with no tour buses to guide them around. Travel all on their own power. The kids were excited, looking over the map as they wanted to make the last day the best one on their trip. All four of them piled around while eating breakfast, surveying their map, looking at a creek they wanted to see and a small store at the end of the hike they would eat lunch at. It was the first day out that they had not packed a full meal with them.

What got to me is with all the activity these four have had, and even with the setbacks, they never seemed to run out of energy for what was needed on any given day. Just being with each other seemed to charge that. They always made it happen even after some slow starts to the days. Packing only a few snacks, water, and a map, they were off again. I looked forward to their return, where they would do the same thing they did all week and come back talking about what they did that day. The kids would always say what their favorite part of the day was with this ritual. They would go on about it for such a long time, still with the energy and innocence kids had at that age, where everything was still fun, and their imaginations ruled everything. It was amazing watching mom and dad smile at these stories; recounting the adventures made this a great experience. Like they said when we left Arizona, this was a trip they would talk about at their kids' weddings.

When they come back from their day, I could hear them conversing as they returned up the hiking trail nearby, talking and carrying on, laughing about the squirrels running around in the trees and the creek they walked by. The fish they saw in the water and birds that flew above them. It was the part of the day when there were still a good two hours before the sun went down.

As dad got the fire going, the last of their hotdogs were put on, and all four of them sat on the bench at their site together. Just laughing. They talked about how fast the week went by, and the daughter asked her parents, "Can we do this again next year? This was so much fun!"

The son asked the same question, with just as much enthusiasm and mom and dad told them, "Yes. Absolutely." I knew I would not be on that trip. Still, I truly hoped they would manage to secure a vehicle capable of bringing all the supplies that were needed, but knowing they had so much fun on this trip, so much as wanting to do it again… I could only hope that I was a small part of that.

As the evening was winding up, the kids started to yawn, and mom and dad kept eyeing the tent after a long day. I could tell they were exhausted but doing their best to stay awake. It was one of those days you just did not want to end. It was their last night, and they make the long drive back home the next day. Mom and dad were at the bench, watching their kids by the fire, laughing and playing together.

Looking at the fire, the mom leaned over and quietly said to the dad, "You know, with everything that happened any other family would have given up after a day, stayed in a motel, or even gone home after the first night. Explained to the kids why and we can try again. Not us. We did it. Remember, this is going to be something we talk about at our kids' weddings."

Dad replied "And all the setbacks we went through and the cost, their weddings will be cheaper than this trip!" They both have a quiet laugh about this together. "You are right, though. This is something that we will always remember."

After that moment together, the daughter comes up to the two of them. "Hey, dad, mom," she started slowly, "Can we sleep on top of the tent like we did the first night? Look at the stars and the shapes they make?"

The dad thought about it for a few seconds, the last night of their camping experience together. He looked up quickly to see the sky they had looked at every night on the trip in amazement at how many stars they could see outside there. "Yes, baby, we can do that. Get your brother!"

The daughter yelled out, "Hey! We're going to sleep with the sky tonight!" They fashioned their original tent cover the same as they did the first night, laying it out as smooth as they could on the ground. The tent poles they acquired previously were moved to the side. They served their purpose the previous nights. Their sleeping bags were all laid out next to each other. The son grabbed the last box of graham crackers to share between them all. In less than a few minutes, the four of them were all lying next to each other, looking up at the sky. All of them picked out shapes from the stars, only slightly obstructed by the smoke from what remained of the campfire. The smell of overpriced burning wood, the occasional crack the fire had on it.

I listened to them pick out objects in the stars, their imaginations running wild. Nobody picked out constellations that were recorded, and nobody cared. I sure as hell did not. At that time, all that mattered to them was seeing what they saw. They created that experience together. All four of them were smiling, laughing, and making references to how stars took the shape of a cow or a building; the son even said he saw a chainsaw in the sky from the shape of the stars. They all laughed at it. For that time, they all had the imagination of children, even mom and dad. They were so happy. It lasted for over an hour until the kids fell asleep. Tired from the day, but a good day. They fell asleep between mom and dad, kids using them as a shield to keep warm.

Not wanting to wake them, the dad looked over at mom, speaking quietly said, "You know, this is the best thing we could have ever done. We will remember this forever. I love you so much. I love our family so much."

The mom, keeping her voice just as quiet, said, "I love you too. We have one thing, so many other people have, the perfect family." They both sat quietly, their hands held together above the kids, not waking them. Just smiling at each other. "We could never recreate this trip. Ever. Look at them."

The dad, still holding mom's hand giving a glance at their kids, passed out from the day, said, "Trip of a lifetime."

Soon after, the mom and dad fell asleep, lying on top of their tent the same they did the first night, under the same stars. Next to their kids.

I have always loved people telling each other "I love you." As many times as I heard it, it never gets old. And I will never get tired of people living their lives together.

As they drifted off to sleep, I took stock of my situation. As a car based in Arizona, it was probably not too likely I would have made a trip up this far. Most people would fly. Or have gotten the van they reserved, at least. It was nice to see the beauty of this park. To see this entire landscape and how it was like nothing I had ever seen. How vast and natural it all was. The sounds the forest makes, the smell of rain here. To spend time with this family and watch them fight some odds on what could have turned into a horrible trip, they made it happen. Not only to create memories for their kids but just that connection as an entire family they had because of this. How that makes them just a little bit stronger. But I took pride in this family. With all they had against them to make this a terrible adventure, they still did it. They made it happen. They never once were short with each other, yelled at each other, or blamed each other. Annoyed by their circumstances, sure. But they never let that stand in the way of having a good time together. They just made it happen and had a great experience. There they were, asleep under millions of stars together. All I could think was a promise to them, I will get them all home safe the next day.

They woke up early the next morning, their final time at the park. There were no hikes that day, no new trails to be conquered. No new adventures. The agenda was the long and ambitious goal of making it all the way back to Arizona in one sprint all the way back. Fifteen to sixteen hours without stops other than bathroom breaks and quick stops for food. Breakfast was easy, some fruit and granola bars. The dad ate two of the left-over hotdogs from the other night. Mom was appeased by an abundant amount of coffee.

All of them finished up the food they had remaining, and they packed up as quickly as they could in the daunting task of trying to fit what they had back into me. Not a square inch went unused. Same as the trip up. The dad used some of the water to put out the last of the coals from the fire the previous night that was still giving a light red and white glow. The steam from the water being applied made a hissing sound, meaning this was it. The end of the trip. They took a walk around their site, being sure to pick up any tiny piece of trash, leaving it in better shape than they had come to it. I had learned this was what the responsible campers do. Lastly, they took a couple of final pictures together at the campsite. Good on them.

With the car packed and the site cleaned, they all looked back at it. The place they called home the last week. All four of them were pretty silent at this, from what I could assume, thinking about the fun they had. The memories they made and how quickly the time went by. The kids only made small talk, bringing back up the favorite parts of their site, sleeping under the stars, cooking food on fire, and the large tree next to where they set up their tent. The tree on the last day they named Wyatt. Yeah, this was it. Getting in those final few minutes. I was glad I was able to see this, and glad I was able to see this with this family. To watch them take on the challenge of a trip like this, clearly unprepared as campers, but wanting to come back and do it again. To give their kids that experience and to strengthen themselves as a family.

With that, they got into me all four of them waived at the campsite to give it a final farewell.

11.

My Conclusion

Well, this is it. Last chapter of this existence. I hit my usable lifespan as a rental car. Done. Put out to pasture. My mileage and condition are all detailed and noted with haphazard documentation. A quick scrub through the automatic car washing bay that never really worked correctly. Final paperwork is tossed on my passenger seat with a sold notice. It reminded me of that large road atlas that sat there not too long back on that same seat a while back. This experience has concluded. Time for the next part of my life. The next phase.

I do wonder what is next. Am I going to a young family, child booster in the back seat to live a life of soccer games and fetching groceries with kids throwing up on the now slightly worn interior? Am I going to sit in traffic every morning and afternoon getting someone to work, coffee cup constantly in the cup holder living the corporate life bitching about going to their job, wearing an ill-fitted golf shirt with the company logo on it? Will a retired couple buy me and live out a few years taking trips and seeing new things? Or do I go to that young person who buys me knowing that I will start every morning as they forge their way through life and make an impact on their world? Maybe the college student? I did not know. Much of what I have learned from people is that you do not know what is in front of you. Plan everything and the universe has different plans. There are no guarantees and no way to know what happens next. You just strap in and enjoy the ride. Just see what happens. We all expire at some point. Even cars. Might as well have fun doing it.

That is what I am looking forward to. The next journey. My next story. The tag is slapped on the windshield for me to be sold. No more rentals. All done. No longer a brand-new blue four-door sedan with a pristine tan interior. It is still there, just used with stories. A little over 52,000 miles of memories on me. The factory warranty was no longer in place. As hard as a lot of it has been, what a great life so far! More dings and scratches, a chip on the windshield, and I really, really need a new air filter. Nobody ever found that hair clip hidden in that small space atop of my trunk interior. I hope nobody ever does. My interior stinks from the hundreds of asses that have sat in me. I hope somebody really cleans the rest of the dried deer blood out of my trunk that was never taken care of properly.

A lot of what I learned from people is to enjoy life. Enjoy what comes to you. Your paint dings, your spills, and even getting pissed on tells a story and make you who you are. I never thought I would start out as a rental car, but here we are. Knowing what I know and experiencing what I have, I do not think I would change it. It has made me who I am today. What a great ride all of this has been...

Final Thoughts

I hope you had fun reading this, or at least made you think about having some fun and enjoying life more. Maybe this has you contemplating about taking that road trip you always wanted to do? As I mentioned at the beginning of this, the whole idea of putting this together came to me when I was coming home from a road trip with my brother, Rick. It was the same trip home we had taken so many times before from Las Vegas, Nevada back to Phoenix, Arizona. My home. Every trip I took with him that I will always cherish. I have never had a bad time with him. Time is never wasted with people you enjoy being around.

At this point in my life, all I care about are people and experiences. I aim to impress exactly nobody anymore, but I will spend some time trying to make anyone laugh. Watching people have a genuine laugh always does me good. Good for them too. Everybody wins. What I wrote is complete fiction; very few parts of this journey are based on things that I may or may not have very, very loosely experienced in my life. Or not. It does not matter.

My goal of writing this was to challenge myself to a new medium I have never done before. Become a writer. Publish a book. Hopefully, create something people will enjoy. This was a period of my life where I needed to do that. Just do something. Create something positive. Writing has never come naturally to me. It was a skill I had to craft with my own signature over the years. My own style. One I could be proud of and live with. This is a story I am proud of writing, giving life and a story to a rental car. Something a lot of people overlook when they travel. The rental car. Reading this means I made it happen. I hope I did it right.

In composing this, I hope anyone who reads this took something from it. A laugh, maybe. Thinking back on something you did twenty years ago. A time you could talk about a trip you took with people and think back on it and feel like you are right there again. Those family vacations. The wedding you drove out of state to attend. A time that you only worried about the road in front of you, even if that was for a new experience. If it challenged you to spend more time with people in your life and know the importance of that, then I would say my job is done. Maybe I did succeed at this whole writing thing. I win. If not, I already got your money anyway. I still win.

Take that trip. Do it. Your kids will only be young for so long. You will be only young for so long. Do not think about it; just do it. Make that memory with your spouse. With your buddy. Your dog. By yourself. Go see the ocean. See the ocean again. See the ocean again if you want. Read that over again, go to the ocean. Take a second honeymoon without thinking much about it. Take a honeymoon every year, even if it is local. Who cares? Fuck it. Go gamble in Las Vegas, conservatively, of course. They do not pay for those casinos by giving money away. See that concert in another state. Drive the highways. Go to that state park. Challenge yourself to travel to somewhere you would never go to. Go camp. Open the windows and experience something new. Take that hike. See what is important to you. Ask that pretty girl/guy to come along. Go to that festival. Drive out and go visit that old friend. Even if you cannot take a long trip, hop in your car and drive somewhere close that is new. Do it now. Do it while you can.

There is never going to be a perfect time. There is always an excuse not to go. Silence that excuse, make it happen. You only get one life, one opportunity to make it truly yours. One existence. Make it exceptional. On that journey, if you should have a rental car, thank them for it. Just a quick tap on the hood or dashboard and some appreciation to the car for getting you there and back. It tells their story too.

Thank You

As cliché as it sounds, I do want to thank my friends and family. I would not be who I am without all of you. I truly, truly mean that. You all are encouraging, supportive, and bring so much to my life. I am not naming specific people, because that would be an entire book to do so. If you are in my life, then I thank you. Only two exceptions to this that I feel the need to mention. These exceptions are only specific to this book.

Regarding this soon-to-be-best-seller that will allow me to retire like a Saudi Prince (fingers crossed), I must thank my friend Dave. You pushed me in the most positive way to create something. To put something out in the world that challenged me and may be something that others will enjoy. Without you keeping up on this and all the support you have given me to do this at a really difficult but awakening point in my life, I do not think I would have finished this. I truly thank you. More than any words I could write here. I suppose if I paid your restaurant tab one night, including an appetizer for you and your family, that might prove my appreciation, and we then call it square. If not, just steal something from my house the next time you are over. Thank you for staying on my ass and the countless hours on the phone with me bouncing all sorts of ideas off you. Thank you for pointing me in the direction for all the resources I needed to do this. This probably would not have been completed without that positive encouragement. To quote, what probably made me go through with this was when you said one sentence. "Create only positives in life." I hope I did you well. Take that from Dave. Create only positives in life.

For what it is worth, I want to thank my dog. His name is Spencer. I can see everyone passing over this paragraph and would not blame you for it. Unless you have the paperback version of this and you are stuck on a plane trip with nothing else to do with twenty-three minutes before you land. Have to pass the time somehow, right? He is an indescribable breed of an animal. When he became a member of my house and went in for the first vet exam, I asked, "What the hell kind of dog is this?"

The Veterinarian, doing the best she could, looking at him with surgical precision, was only able to respond by saying, "I. Do. Not. Know." He is a mutt but has a huge heart. And tiny little legs. Huge ears. While it may be unconventional to thank a dog, I stand by this. I wrote this entire book in my living room with him. When I pet him and ask his opinion on my work, reading it over and over to him, he is quite happy, shaking his ass and wagging his tail like it is the best thing he has ever heard. When he sleeps on the couch or my chair, he looks up for a minute, sleepy-eyed, and goes back to his slumber when presented with the same questions. But he always looks up when I ask him to listen to me reading a chapter to him. He was with the conception of this book until the end. He just likes spending time with me. I liked spending time with him writing this. It is something I will always remember about him long after he is gone. Creating this with him. Some things just cannot be put into words, and this is one of them. Spencer deserves his credit.

Take that trip. I dare you. Travel. Now. Do it.

-Jim McAllister